KANE

MATT AND TOM OLDFIELD

ULTIMATE FOOTBALL HEROES

KANE

FROM THE PLAYGROUND
TO THE PITCH

DINO

First published by Dino Books in 2017,
An imprint of Bonnier Books UK,
The Plaza,
535 Kings Road,
London SW10 0SZ

🐦 @dinobooks
🐦 @footieheroesbks
www.heroesfootball.com
www.bonnierbooks.co.uk

Design and typesetting by www.envydesign.co.uk

Paperback ISBN: 978 1 78606 886 6
E-book ISBN: 978 1 78606 912 2

British Library cataloguing-in-publication data:
A catalogue record for this book is available from the british library.

Printed and bound in Great Britain by Clays Lltd, Elcograf S.p.A.

10

For Noah and Nico,
Southampton's future strikeforce

ULTIMATE
FOOTBALL HEROES

Matt Oldfield is an accomplished writer and the editor-in-chief of football review site *Of Pitch & Page*. Tom Oldfield is a freelance sports writer and the author of biographies on Cristiano Ronaldo, Arsène Wenger and Rafael Nadal.

Cover illustration by Dan Leydon.
To learn more about Dan visit danleydon.com
To purchase his artwork visit etsy.com/shop/footynews
Or just follow him on Twitter @danleydon

TABLE OF CONTENTS

ACKNOWLEDGEMENTS

First of all, I'd like to thank John Blake Publishing –
and particularly my editor James Hodgkinson – for
giving me the opportunity to work on these books
and for supporting me throughout. Writing stories for
the next generation of football fans is both an honour
and a pleasure.

I wouldn't be doing this if it wasn't for my brother,
Tom. I owe him so much and I'm very grateful for
his belief in me as an author. I feel like Robin setting
out on a solo career after a great partnership with
Batman. I hope I do him (Tom, not Batman) justice
with these new books.

Next up, I want to thank my friends for keeping

me sane during long hours in front of the laptop. Pang, Will, Mills, Doug, John, Charlie – the laughs and the cups of coffee are always appreciated.

I've already thanked my brother but I'm also very grateful to the rest of my family, especially Melissa, Noah and of course Mum and Dad. To my parents, I owe my biggest passions: football and books. They're a real inspiration for everything I do.

Finally, I couldn't have done this without Iona's encouragement and understanding during long, work-filled weekends. Much love to you.

CHAPTER 1

ENGLAND HERO

Thursday, 5 October 2017

In the Wembley tunnel, Harry closed his eyes and soaked up the amazing atmosphere. He was back at the home of football, the stadium where he had first achieved his childhood dream of playing for England. 19 March 2015, England vs Lithuania – he remembered that game like it was yesterday. He had scored that day and now, with England facing Slovenia, he needed to do it again. As England's captain and Number 9, it was his job to shoot them to the 2018 World Cup.

'Come on, lads!' Harry called out to his teammates behind him: friends like Joe Hart, Kyle Walker and

Eric Dier. It was a real honour to be their leader.
With a victory over Slovenia, they would all be on
their way to the biggest tournament of their lives
in Russia.

Harry looked down at the young mascot by his
side and smiled at him. 'Right, let's do this!'

As the two of them led the England team out onto
the pitch, the fans clapped and cheered. Harry didn't
look up at the thousands of faces and flags; instead,
he looked down at the grass in front of him. He
was totally focused on his task: scoring goals and
beating Slovenia.

'If you get a chance, test the keeper,' Harry said
to his partners in attack, Raheem Sterling and
Marcus Rashford, before kick-off. 'I'll be there for the
rebound!'

Harry's new Premiership season with Tottenham
Hotspur had not begun well in August, but by
September he was back to his lethal best. That
month alone, he scored an incredible thirteen goals,
including two goals for England against Malta. He
could score every type of goal – tap-ins, headers, one-

on-ones, long-range shots, penalties, even free kicks. That's what made him such a dangerous striker.

With Slovenia defending well, Harry didn't get many chances in the first half. He got in good positions but the final ball never arrived.

'There's no need to panic yet,' Harry told his teammates in the dressing room. He really didn't want a repeat of England's terrible performance against Iceland at Euro 2016. That match still haunted him. 'We're good enough to win this by playing our natural game. Be patient!'

As Ryan Bertrand dribbled down the left wing, Harry sprinted towards the six-yard box. Ryan's cross didn't reach him but the ball fell to Raheem instead. His shot was going in until a defender deflected it wide.

'Unlucky!' Harry shouted, putting his hands on his head. 'Keep going, we're going to score!'

Without this kind of strong self-belief, Harry would never have made it to the top of European football. There had been lots of setbacks along the way: rejections, disappointments and bad form. But every time, Harry bounced back with crucial goals at crucial moments. That's what made him such a superstar.

A matter of seconds later, a rebound fell to him on the edge of the penalty area. Surely, this was his moment. He pulled back his left foot and curled a powerful shot towards the bottom corner. The fans were already up on their feet, ready to celebrate. Harry never missed… but this time he did. The ball flew just wide of the post. Harry couldn't believe it. He looked up at the sky and sighed.

On the sideline, England manager Gareth Southgate cheered his team on. 'That's much better – the goal is coming, lads!'

But after ninety minutes, the goal still hadn't come. The fourth official raised his board: eight minutes of injury time.

'It's not over yet, boys!' Harry shouted, to inspire his teammates.

The Slovenian goalkeeper tried to throw the ball out to his left-back but Kyle got there first. Straight away, Harry was on the move from the back post to the front post. After playing together for years at Tottenham, they knew how to score great goals.

As Kyle crossed it in, Harry used his burst of speed to get in front of the centre-back. Again, the England supporters stood and waited anxiously. The ball was perfect and Harry stretched out his long right leg to meet it. The keeper got a touch on his shot but he couldn't keep it out.

Goooooooooooooaaaaaaaaaaaaaaaaaaalllllllllllllllllllll llllll!!!!!!!!!!!!!!!!!!!!!

He had done it! Joy, relief, pride – Harry felt every emotion as he ran towards the fans. This time, he hadn't let them down. He held up the Three Lions on his shirt and screamed until his throat got sore.

'Captain to the rescue!' Kyle laughed as they hugged by the corner flag.

'No, it was all thanks to you!' Harry replied.

At the final whistle, he threw his arms up in the air. It was a phenomenal feeling to qualify for the 2018 World Cup. He couldn't wait to lead England to glory.

'We are off to Russia!' a voice shouted over the loudspeakers and the whole stadium cheered.

It was yet another moment that Harry would never forget. Against the odds, he was making his childhood dreams come true. He was the star striker for Tottenham, the club that he had supported all his life. And now, like his hero David Beckham, he was the captain of England.

Harry had never given up, even when it looked like he wouldn't make it as a professional footballer. With the support of his family and his coaches, and lots of hard work and dedication, he had proved everyone wrong to become a world-class goal machine.

It had been an incredible journey from Walthamstow to Wembley, and Harry was only just getting started.

CHAPTER 2

ALWAYS KICKING

'Mum!' Charlie shouted, stamping his feet.

Kim sighed and put her magazine down. 'What's happened now?'

'I spent ages building a Lego tower and Harry just kicked it over,' her older son answered. 'That was *my* tower!'

'I'm sorry, darling, but I'm sure Harry didn't mean it. Your brother doesn't know what he's doing with his little feet yet.'

Harry was nearly two years old and he was always on the move around their house in Walthamstow, North London. He had a few bumps on his head but it was his legs that caused the most trouble. Everywhere he went, they never stopped kicking.

Kim wasn't surprised, though.

'Do you remember before your brother was born when he was still in my tummy?' she asked Charlie as she lifted Harry up onto the sofa. Charlie didn't reply; he was busy building a new tower. 'He was always kicking, even back then, wasn't he? I didn't get a good night's sleep for months!'

Kim held Harry up in the air to give his legs room to swing. 'No, you don't like letting me sleep, do you?' He smiled and wiggled his hands and feet. 'I knew you'd be a boy; there was no doubt about that. I told your Daddy that you were going to be sporty and do you know what he said? He said, "Great, he'll play for TOTTENHAM!"'

Harry's smile grew wider when he heard the name of their local football club. It was a word that his dad, Pat, said so often that it had become his favourite word. The Kane family lived only five miles away from Tottenham's stadium, White Hart Lane.

'Wow, you really love that idea, don't you!' Kim laughed. 'Well, your Grandad Eric was a good footballer in his day. Maybe you'll get his talent, rather than your Dad's. Bless him, he always says that bad injuries ruined his career but I think it was his bad first touch!'

It was a bright, sunny afternoon and so Kim took her two sons out to the local park. Hopefully, after a few hours of open space and fresh air, Charlie and Harry would sleep well that night, and so would their mum. Once they found a shady spot on the grass, Kim lay down the picnic rug and lifted Harry out of the pushchair.

'Charlie, you've got to stay where I can see you!' she called out as he chased after a squirrel.

After doing a few laps of the rug, Harry sat down and looked around him. He saw leaves and twigs and insects. He saw huge trees above him and patches of blue sky in between. Then his eyes fixed on the exciting scene in front of him. A group of kids were playing football with jumpers for goalposts. That looked like fun. He stood up and went over to explore.

'Harry, stop!' Kim shouted. She chased after her son and scooped him up just before he reached the other kids' football game. In her arms, Harry kept watching and his legs kept moving. He was desperate to kick the ball.

'Not today, darling,' his mum said, giving him a kiss on the cheek. 'But soon, I promise!'

*

'So, how was your day?' Pat asked, as they all ate dinner together. After a long day's work at the garage, he loved to come home to his happy family.

Charlie could now feed himself like a grown-up but Harry still needed a high chair and some help. Even with Pat holding the spoon, Harry got strawberry yoghurt all over his hands and face.

'I built an awesome tower but Harry broke it with his silly little feet,' Charlie told his dad. He was looking for sympathy, but Pat had other ideas.

'Good, your brother's getting ready for his big Tottenham career! Football runs in the family, you know. Just ask your Grandad – I was one of Ireland's best young players but sadly…'

Kim rolled her eyes. Not again! She decided not to mention Harry's kicking in the park. It would only get her husband's hopes up even more.

CHAPTER 3

HEROES AT WHITE HART LANE

'Have you been good boys today?' Pat asked his sons one evening as they all ate dinner together.

Charlie and Harry knew the right answer. 'Yes!'

Their dad smiled and reached into his trouser pocket. He took out three rectangles of white card and placed them down on the table. Then he watched and waited for his sons' reactions.

Harry thought he knew what they were but he didn't want to get his hopes up until he was sure. His dad had promised him that he could go to his first Tottenham game once he turned four. For his birthday, he got a Spurs shirt and a Spurs football, but no Spurs ticket. Charlie had been to White Hart Lane a few times and Harry was desperate to join them. Was his dream finally going to come true? There in the top left corner was the important word, written in navy blue – 'Tottenham'. He was right; they *were* match tickets! Harry jumped for joy.

'Wow, thanks!' he said, running over to give his dad a big hug. 'This is the best gift ever!'

Suddenly, Harry and Charlie weren't interested in eating anymore. Instead, they ran around the living room, waving the tickets in the air and chanting, 'We're going to White Hart Lane! We're going to White Hart Lane!'

Kim laughed. 'You'll need to keep a close eye on them,' she warned her husband. 'This is just the start!'

'Yes, I think I'll look after these,' Pat said, taking the tickets back from his over-excited sons.

It was a three o'clock kick-off on Saturday but Harry and Charlie were sitting in their Tottenham shirts at breakfast. They spent the morning playing football in the garden, pretending to be their heroes.

'David Ginola gets the ball on the left,' Charlie began the commentary, 'he dribbles past one defender and then another. Look at that skill! He's just outside the penalty area now, he looks up and...'

Harry didn't like playing in goal against his brother. He hardly ever made a save because Charlie's shots were too powerful.

...*Goooooooooooooooooooaaaaaaaaaalllllllllllllllllllllll lllllllllllll!!!!!!!!!!!!!!!!!!!!*

Charlie ran towards the corner of the garden and celebrated by pulling his Spurs shirt over his head.

'Right, my turn!' Harry said, picking up the ball.

His number one hero, Teddy Sheringham, had just left Tottenham to sign for Manchester United. But Harry already had his new favourite – German Jürgen Klinsmann. It was a hard name for a four-year-old to say but Harry did his best.

'Kiman runs towards the penalty area...'

He needed to strike the ball perfectly if he wanted to score past his older brother. Harry looked up at the goal and kicked it as hard as he could. The ball bounced and skipped towards the bottom corner...

...*Goooooooooooooooooooaaaaaaaaaaaaaalllllllllllllll lllllllllllll!!!!!!!!!!!!!!!!!!!!*

Normally, Harry celebrated with the Klinsmann dive but his Spurs shirt was white and he couldn't make his White Hart Lane debut wearing a muddy shirt! So instead, he jumped up and pumped his fist. He could tell that it was going to be a very good day.

After lunch, it was finally time for them to leave.

'Have you got your hats?' Kim asked at the front door.

Harry nodded.

'Gloves?'

Harry nodded.

'Good, stay close to your dad and have a great time!'

They were off! Harry couldn't wait to get to White Hart Lane. On the bus, he imagined the people, the noise, the goals. As they crossed through the Walthamstow reservoirs, Charlie had a thought.

'Dad, have you got the tickets?'

There was panic on Pat's face as he checked all of his pockets, once and then twice. 'Oh dear,' he muttered.

Harry's face dropped with disappointment. How had his dad forgotten the tickets? Why hadn't he checked before they left?

Suddenly, a smile spread across Pat's face, and he held up the tickets. 'Just kidding!' he cheered.

'Dad, don't scare us like that!' Harry shouted. He didn't find the joke funny at all.

When they got off the bus, the stadium was right there in front of them. Harry stood there looking up, his mouth wide open. It was even bigger than he'd expected.

'Come on, let's go in and find our seats!' his dad said. 'Don't let go of my hand, okay? If you get lost, Mum won't ever let us come back.'

Harry held on tightly as they moved through the crowds towards the turnstile, on their way to their seats. There were so many people everywhere and so much to see and hear.

'Get today's match programme here!' the sellers shouted.

Some Tottenham fans talked about their players in between bites of burgers and hot dogs. Other

Tottenham fans were already singing songs even before they entered the stadium. It was all so exciting.

Once they were through the turnstile, Harry could see a square of green in the distance. His eyes lit up – the pitch! As they got closer, he couldn't believe the size of it. How did the players keep running from box to box for ninety minutes? It looked impossible.

'Look, there's Ginola!' Charlie shouted, pointing down at the players warming up. 'And there's Klinsmann!'

Harry stood up on his seat to get a better view. He was in the same stadium as his heroes; it didn't get any better than that.

Tottenham, Tottenham!

As the players ran out of the tunnel for the start of the game, the noise grew even louder. Spurs needed a win to stay out of the relegation zone. After a few minutes, Ginola got the ball on the left wing.

'Come on!' the Tottenham fans cheered, rising to their feet.

Ginola curled a brilliant cross into the penalty area. Harry held his breath as Klinsmann stretched to reach it…

*Goooooooooooooooooooooaaaaaaaaaaaaaaaaaalllll
lllllllllllllllllllll!!!!!!!!!!!!!!!!!!!*

What a start! Harry and Charlie jumped up and down together, cheering for their heroes.

The rest of the match was very tense but Tottenham held on for the victory. By the final whistle, Harry was exhausted but very happy. He was already looking forward to his next trip to White Hart Lane.

'So, who was man of the match?' Pat asked his sons on the bus home.

'Ginola!' Charlie replied.

'Klinsmann!' Harry replied.

Their dad shook his head. 'If we ever keep a clean sheet, it's always the goalkeeper!'

CHAPTER 4

RIDGEWAY ROVERS

'Why do we have to leave?' Charlie cried out. 'It's not fair. This is our home!'

Their parents had just given them some terrible news; the family was moving from Walthamstow to Chingford. They had never even heard of Chingford.

'We'll have more space there,' Kim replied. 'You'll have bigger bedrooms and a bigger football pitch in the garden too.'

'Look, we're not talking about Australia!' Pat said. 'Chingford is only a few miles away.'

'But all our friends are *here*,' Charlie argued.

As the conversation carried on, Harry had an important question to ask: 'How far is it from White Hart Lane?'

'It's only five miles away, the same distance as now.'

Kim and Pat finally won the family argument with a killer fact: David Beckham had grown up in Chingford.

'Really?' Harry asked excitedly. After the 1998 World Cup, Beckham was England's most famous footballer. Despite his red card versus Argentina, every kid in the country wanted to look and play like Becks.

His dad nodded. 'He played for a local team called Ridgeway Rovers.'

'Cool, can I play for Ridgeway Rovers too?'

'It's a deal!' Kim said, looking relieved.

Harry was determined to become a star striker for Tottenham and England, especially after visiting White Hart Lane. He practised all the time, with whatever he could find. In the garden and the park, he played with his own real football. It was his pride and joy, and he looked after it carefully. In the street, he played with any can or bottle that he could find. In the house, he swapped his football for rolled-up socks.

'STOP KICKING THINGS!' Charlie shouted angrily from through his bedroom door.

'Sorry!' Harry replied quickly, running downstairs to help with dinner. He had been using his brother's door as a shooting target again. He knew that it wasn't allowed but he just couldn't help himself.

'Can I join Ridgeway Rovers now?' Harry asked his parents as they sat down to eat. He was desperate to test his talent against real opponents on a real pitch.

Pat knew that his son wasn't going to give up until it was sorted. Fifteen minutes later, he returned to the living room with good news. 'The Ridgeway Rovers trials are coming up in a couple of weeks. I'll take you along.'

'Thanks!' Harry cheered. He couldn't wait to follow in Becks' footsteps. But first, he had lots more practice to do.

'It's great to see so many of you down here,' Dave Bricknell, the Ridgeway Rovers coach, told the eager young faces at Loughton Rugby Club. 'Welcome! Today, we're looking for brilliant new players to join our club, but most importantly, we're going to have some fun, yes?'

'YES!' Harry cheered with the other boys.

As they all practised passing in pairs, Dave walked around the pitch. He was looking for a nice touch, as well as accuracy and power in the pass.

'Very good!' he called out to Harry.

Next up was dribbling. It wasn't Harry's favourite skill but he managed to keep the ball under control as he weaved in and out of the cones. He was relieved when it was over and he had only knocked one over.

'Right, it's the moment you've all been waiting for,' Dave said to the group. 'Shooting! Do we have a goalkeeper here?'

Everyone looked around but no-one stepped forward.

The coach looked surprised. 'Really? Not a single keeper?'

Harry was really looking forward to scoring some goals but he also didn't mind playing in goal, especially if it wasn't Charlie who was shooting at him. Slowly, he raised his arm.

'Great! What's your name?' Dave asked.

'Harry.'

'Thanks, Harry! You'll get a chance to shoot later on, I promise.'

He put on a pair of gloves, walked over to the goal and waited. As the first shot came towards him, he didn't even have to move. He caught the ball and rolled it to the side. The next shot was better and he had to throw himself across the goal to tip it round the post.

'What a save, Harry!' Dave clapped. 'I think we've found our new keeper!'

Harry enjoyed diving around but he didn't want to be Ian Walker or David Seaman. He wanted to be Teddy Sheringham or Jürgen Klinsmann.

'Coach,' he called out after the first round of shots, 'I don't really play in goal. I normally play outfield as a striker.'

'Not again!' Dave thought to himself. Young keepers always got bored and asked to move to attack for the glory. Even so, he made a promise to the boy:

'No problem, I'll put you up front for the match at the end. You're a natural in goal, though!'

Harry waited patiently for his chance to shine. It took a little while, even once the match had started. But finally, his teammate kicked a long pass down the pitch and he was off, sprinting as fast as his little legs could go. He wasn't the fastest but he had a head start because of his clever run.

Harry beat the defender to the ball, took one touch to control it and calmly placed his shot in the bottom corner.

Goooooooooooooooooooaaaaaaaaaaaaaaaaalllllllllllllll llllllllllllllllll!!!!!!!!!!!!!!!!!!

Ten minutes later, Harry had a hat-trick and a place in the Ridgeway Rovers team.

'You're a natural keeper *and* a natural striker,' Dave laughed. 'I guess you're just a natural footballer!'

Harry couldn't wait for the real matches to begin. As he stepped out onto the field for the first time in the blue and white Ridgeway Rovers shirt, he felt unstoppable. This was it. He was ready for the big time, but was the big time ready for him?

When the ball came to him in the penalty area, Harry took a shot and it deflected off a defender and out for a corner.

'I'll take it!' Harry shouted, chasing over to the flag.

It was a long way from the corner to the penalty area, so he kicked it as hard as he could. The ball flew over the heads of everyone, including the goalkeeper. It landed in the back of the net.

Goooooooooooooooaaaaaaaaaaaaaaaaalllllllllllllllllllllllll llllllll!!!!!!!!!!!!!!!!!!!!!!

Harry punched the air with joy – he was off the mark on his debut! It was a lucky strike but that didn't matter. Would he ever get tired of scoring goals? He really didn't think so.

CHAPTER 5

FOOTBALL, FOOTBALL, FOOTBALL

'That's it! Keep your head steady and lean over the ball as you kick it.'

At the weekends, Harry's dad often helped him with extra training in the back garden. There was so much that he wanted to improve, especially his shooting. He couldn't relax if he wanted to keep his place as Ridgeway Rovers' number one striker.

'Right, I think that's enough,' Pat said after an hour. 'You've got a game later today and you'll be too tired to score.'

'Okay, just three more shots,' Harry begged.

If his dad was busy, he went to the park with Charlie. When Harry was younger, his older brother used to make him stand between two trees and try to save his powerful shots for hours. That wasn't much fun but now that he was eight, Charlie let him join in properly. If there were other kids around, they'd play a big match but if it was just the two of them, they had long, competitive one-on-one battles. Harry was a skilful footballer but his older brother had one weapon that could defeat him: strength.

'Come on, that's not fair!' Harry shouted as he picked himself up off the grass. 'You can't just push me off the ball like that.'

Charlie shrugged. 'That was a shoulder-to-shoulder challenge. It's not my fault that I'm bigger than you.'

It was no use complaining; Harry just had to find other ways to beat his brother. Luckily, he was very determined. A few times he stormed off angrily but most of the time, Harry tried and tried until he succeeded.

'You're definitely getting better, bro!' Charlie told him as they walked back home together for lunch.

Harry smiled proudly; that was his aim. He didn't want to just be an average player; he wanted to become a great player like his Tottenham heroes. He didn't care how much time and effort that would take. Harry played football before school, at break-time, at lunchtime, and then after school too.

'See you later, Mum!' he called out as he gulped down a glass of water and threw his bag down.

Kim didn't need to ask where her son was going. She knew exactly where he would be and what he'd be doing. 'Just be careful and make sure you're back for dinner,' was all she said.

In the summer, Harry and his friends played in the park all day. But in the winter, it was too dark so they swapped grass for tarmac. Under the streetlights, their games could go on much longer, although there were more obstacles to deal with.

'Stop!' Harry called out. 'Car coming!'

All shots had to be low and soft. A few broken flowers were fine but broken windows meant game over.

'Kev, don't blast it!'

'Mrs Curtis is watching at the curtain!'

Harry loved their street games because they really

helped him to improve his technique. In the tight space between the pavements, his control had to be excellent and he had to look up quickly to find the pass. His movement had to be good too if he wanted to escape from the defenders and score.

'Yes!' he would scream as he made a sudden run towards goal. If he got it right, his marker wouldn't have time to turn and catch him.

Harry's hero, Teddy Sheringham, was back as Tottenham's Number 10. He watched him carefully in every match and tried to copy his movement. Teddy wasn't the quickest striker in the Premier League but he was always alert and clever around the penalty area.

'Stay tight on Harry,' his opponents would say. 'Don't switch off or he'll score!'

Normally, their street games were friendly and fun, but not always. If the result came down to next goal wins, everyone took it very seriously.

'No way! That went straight over the jumper – that's not a goal.'

'What are you talking about? That was post and in!'

'Stop cheating!'

'You're the one who's cheating!'

Of course, there was no referee, so Harry often had to be the peacemaker. He wanted to win just as much as the other boys, if not more, but he always stayed calm. Getting angry didn't help anyone. If Harry ended up on the losing team one day, he just worked even harder the next day.

Harry's days started and ended with football. It was all he thought about. In bed, he lay there imagining his Tottenham debut:

It was 0–0 with ten minutes to go and he came on to replace Les Ferdinand up front. Darren Anderton got the ball in midfield and played a brilliant through-ball. Harry ran towards goal, and he was one-on-one with the goalkeeper. Could he stay calm and find the net?

Unfortunately, he fell asleep before he found out the answer.

CHAPTER 6

ARSENAL

Harry was used to seeing Premier League scouts at Ridgeway Rovers matches. There was lots of young talent in north east London and no club wanted to miss out on the next David Beckham. If he kept scoring, Harry believed that it could be him.

'Well played, today,' said Ian Marshall, the Chairman of Ridgeway Rovers, as he ruffled the boy's short hair. 'How many is that for the season now?'

Harry pretended to count but he knew the answer. 'Eighteen in fifteen games.'

'You're our little Alan Shearer!'

Harry shook his head. 'I prefer Sheringham.'

Ian laughed. 'Of course, Teddy it is then! Do you mind if I have a quick chat with your dad please?'

While Harry practised his keepie-uppies nearby, the adults chatted.

'We had an Arsenal scout here today,' Ian said. 'He wants your boy to go for a trial there.'

Pat wasn't surprised; he already knew that his son was a very good player. But he wanted to do what was best for him.

'What do you think?' he asked Ian. 'He's still only eight – is he too young to join an academy? I want Harry to keep enjoying his football.'

The Ridgeway Rovers coach nodded. 'I understand. Look, I don't think there's any harm in him trying it out. If he doesn't like it, he can just come back here. We'll always have a place for him.'

Pat thanked Ian. 'Harry loves everything about football but I just don't want to get his hopes up. It can be a very cruel business for youngsters.'

As soon as they were in the car, Harry wanted to know everything. 'What were you and Ian talking about?'

'Wait until we get home. I need to talk to your mum first.'

'Okay, but was it a Tottenham scout?'

'Harry!'

'A West Ham scout?'

'HARRY!'

After a whispered chat with Kim in the kitchen, Pat shared the good news with his son. 'Arsenal want to offer you a trial. What do you think?'

Harry's first thoughts were a mix of pride and disappointment. It was amazing news that a Premier League club wanted him, but why did it have to be Arsenal, Tottenham's biggest rivals?

'But we hate Arsenal, Dad!'

Pat laughed. 'We don't really hate them, son. It's just a football rivalry. They're a great club and they're doing very well at the moment.'

His dad was right; Arsenal were the second-best team in England, just behind Manchester United. They had exciting superstars like Dennis Bergkamp, Patrick Vieira and Thierry Henry. Tottenham, meanwhile, were down in mid-table.

That was enough to make Harry change his mind. 'Okay, so when can I start?'

For the big day, Harry decided not to wear his Tottenham shirt. He was already going to be the new kid at Arsenal and he didn't want to make things even harder.

'How are you feeling?' his mum asked on the journey to London Colney, Arsenal's training ground location.

'Fine,' Harry replied but really, he was getting more and more nervous in the backseat of the car. It was going to be a massive challenge for him, and what if he failed? What if he wasn't good enough and made a fool of himself? This wasn't Ridgeway Rovers anymore.

'You'll be brilliant,' Kim told him, giving his hand a squeeze. 'But maybe don't tell your new coaches that you're a Spurs fan straight away!'

Harry smiled and felt a bit more relaxed. As long as he tried his best, what more could he do?

As they drove into the Arsenal Training Centre, Harry couldn't believe his eyes. Compared to Ridgeway's Peter May Sports Centre, it looked like a whole city. There were ten perfect, full-size pitches, as well as lots of indoor facilities.

'Not bad, is it?' his dad joked.

Once the session began, Harry's nerves turned into adrenaline. 'I can do this!' he told himself. Everything felt better with a football at his feet.

In the drills, he showed off his best touch and passing. Some of the other boys had incredible technique already, but Harry didn't let that get him down. He was waiting for his moment to shine – shooting. When that moment arrived, the Arsenal goalkeepers didn't have a chance. Bottom left, top right, straight down the middle; Harry scored every time.

'Great work!' the coach clapped.

That trial session soon turned into a whole season at Arsenal. At first, it felt strange to play for Tottenham's enemies but Harry soon forgot about that. He was having so much fun. He wasn't as skilful as some of his teammates, but that wasn't really his role – he was the one who scored the goals. He didn't play every minute of every match but he tried to make the most of every opportunity.

At the end of the season, the Arsenal academy had to choose which youngsters to keep and which youngsters to let go. Harry crossed his fingers tightly for weeks but unfortunately, it was bad news. The coaches decided that he was too small for his age.

'I'm so sorry,' his dad said, giving him a hug. 'Be proud and keep going. Once you've had your growth spurt, Arsenal are going to regret it!'

For the next few days, Harry was so angry and upset that he wanted to give up. But luckily, that feeling didn't last long. He realised that he loved football too much to stop. If Arsenal didn't want him, he knew another team that hopefully still did.

'Dad, can I go and play for Ridgeway Rovers again?'

The Peter May Sports Centre would always feel like home.

'Welcome back, kid!' Ian said with a wink. 'What we're looking for is a goalscorer, a fox in the box – do you know of anyone like that?'

Harry grinned. 'Yes – me!'

CHAPTER 7

CHINGFORD FOUNDATION SCHOOL

After playing for Ridgeway Rovers, Harry was soon following in David Beckham's footsteps for a second time when he started at Chingford Foundation School. Becks' signed shirt hung proudly in the entrance lobby at Chingford. Harry looked at it every morning as he arrived at school, hoping that it would bring him luck, but especially on the day of the trial for the Year 7 football team. Chingford had one of the best track records in Greater London and Harry was ready to be their next star.

'I'm the striker that they need and I'll show them at the trial,' he told his brother, Charlie, on the way to school. He wasn't quite as confident as he sounded but he was as determined as ever.

Harry loved scoring goals. It was an amazing feeling when a shot hit the back of the net. But he could do a lot more than just that. During his year at Arsenal, he had improved his all-round game. He was good in possession, and creative too. Setting up chances for his teammates was almost as much fun as scoring.

'Just don't be too selfish,' Charlie warned. 'Mr Leadon hates a show-off!'

Harry didn't forget his brother's advice. After changing into his white Tottenham shirt, he made his way out onto the pitch with the other boys.

'Good luck!' Harry told his mates. They were all competing for places now.

After a warm-up and some passing exercises, Mark Leadon, Chingford's football coach, split the boys up and gave half of them orange bibs.

'I'm looking for team players today,' he told them. 'If you just want to show off how many tricks you can do, go do that in the playground. I want to see how you can work together and help each other to win. Right, let's play!'

Most of Harry's schoolmates knew that he was a good footballer because they had seen him play in the lunchtime games. They knew that he had played for Arsenal, but he was still quite small and he didn't have the flashy skills and speed to dribble past everyone. There were other boys who looked more talented but Harry hadn't played at his best. Yet.

'If we pass the ball around, they'll get tired and the chances will come,' he told his teammates. He had made himself the leader.

Harry was ready to be patient but he didn't need to be. The opposition defenders couldn't cope with his clever runs into space. As the cross came in, he made a late run to beat his marker to the ball.

Goooooooooooooooooaaaaaaaaaaaaaaaaaaaallllllllllllllll llllllllllllll!!!!!!!!!!!!!!!!!!!

Harry didn't run off and celebrate on his own; he ran straight to thank the teammate who had set him up. Together, they ran back for the restart. They had more goals to score.

'I like this kid,' Mark thought to himself on the sidelines. 'For an eleven-year-old, he really understands football. He knows where to go and he knows where his teammates are going to go too.'

Harry didn't stop running until Mark blew the whistle to end the game. By then, it had turned into a thrashing. When he found room to shoot, Harry shot and scored. When he could see another player in space, he passed for them to score instead. He was involved in every part of his team's victory.

They walked off the pitch together, with their arms around each other's shoulders. Their man of the match was right at the centre of the gang.

'Well played,' Mark said to them but he was looking straight at Harry.

'Thanks, sir,' he replied politely, but inside, he was buzzing with pride.

Mark was very impressed. Every year, he had excellent young footballers in his school team but this boy seemed special. He had technique, vision, movement *and* work-rate. Mark could tell that it was going to be a good season.

'So, how did it go?' Charlie asked when his brother got home from school that evening.

Harry smiled and shrugged modestly. 'It went okay, I think.'

Harry became the first name on a very successful teamsheet. His goals led Chingford to school cup glory.

'If you keep working hard, your shirt could be hanging up there with Becks one day!' Mark Leadon told him.

CHAPTER 8

HEROES AND DREAMS

'Welcome!' David Beckham announced to a group of sixteen boys and girls. The England superstar was in East London to launch his brand-new football academy. With his white Adidas tracksuit and trendy haircut, he looked so cool. 'Today, we're going to practise some of my favourite skills.'

Harry wasn't really listening; he was too busy staring at his hero. He was one of the Chingford Foundation School footballers who had been selected to go to the academy launch. So now, Becks was right next to him, giving him football tips! Surely, it was too good to be true? But no, it was really happening.

Like Becks, Harry wore an Adidas tracksuit, but their hairstyles didn't match. Harry's head was shaved short, like Becks way back in 2000, but Becks had tried five different looks since then! Harry felt very nervous. Not only was Becks watching him but there were also cameras everywhere. Still, he was desperate to impress. Harry dribbled the ball carefully from end to end, and kept his keepie-uppies simple.

'That's it, great work everyone!' Becks called out.

At the end of the day, he shook each of them by the hand and chatted with them. When it was Harry's turn, he was too nervous and shy to speak. Luckily, Becks went first.

'Well done today. Are you one of the lads from Chingford?' he asked.

Harry nodded. 'A-and I play for Ridgeway Rovers too.'

Becks smiled. 'Great club, so what's next? What's your dream?'

Harry didn't need to think about that one. 'I want to play for England at Wembley!'

'Good choice, it's the best feeling in the world. If you keep working hard, you can do it. Good luck!'

As Harry travelled home with his mum, he could still hear his hero's inspirational words in his head – 'you can do it'.

*

'Play the pass now!' Harry shouted, as he sprinted towards goal. It was only one of their street games, but that didn't matter. Every football match was important. The pass never arrived, however.

'Car!' one of his mates shouted, picking up the ball.

As he moved over towards the pavement, Harry noticed two strange things about this particular car. Firstly, it wasn't the typical old banger that usually drove through the area. It was a huge black Range Rover and it looked brand-new. Secondly, the car didn't speed off once they were out of the way. Instead, it stopped and the driver's door opened.

'Hey guys, do you fancy a game?' the man said with a big smile on his face.

Harry's jaw dropped. Was he dreaming? Was

Jermain Defoe, Spurs' star striker, really standing there asking to play with them?

'Yes, Jermain's on our team!'

'Hey, that's not fair!'

After a few minutes of arguing, the decision was made: Harry and Jermain would play on opposite teams.

'Let's see what you've got!' Jermain told him with a wink.

Harry loved a challenge but this one was impossible. He knew that he couldn't compete with a top Premier League striker yet but he did his best. He chased every pass and got on the ball as often as possible. He wanted to show off all his skills.

When he wasn't racing around the pitch, Harry tried to watch his superstar opponent in action. Jermain scored lots of goals but Harry was more interested in the rest of his play. With a powerful burst of speed, he could escape from any tackle. Jermain was always thinking one step ahead, playing quick passes to get his teammates into really dangerous areas. If there was a loose ball, or a goalmouth scramble, he was always the first to react.

First Becks and now Jermain; Harry was learning from the very best.

After half an hour, Jermain had to leave. 'Thanks for the game, lads!'

The boys all stood and watched as the black Range Rover drove away. Then they looked at each other, their faces full of wonder. It was a night that none of them would ever forget.

'They're not going to believe us at school, are they?' Harry said.

His mates shook their heads. 'Not in a million years.'

CHAPTER 9

TOTTENHAM AT LAST

'I can't believe you're leaving us again,' Ian Marshall said with a wink and a handshake. 'I hope it goes well for you, lad, but if not, just come back home!'

Harry would miss playing for Ridgeway Rovers but Watford had offered him a trial. They weren't as big as Arsenal or Tottenham, but they were a good Championship team. It was the sort of new challenge that he needed.

'Good luck!' Pat called from the car window as he dropped Harry off at the Watford training centre. His son hadn't said much during the journey and he hoped that he wasn't brooding on his experience at

Arsenal. Harry was at a different club now and there was nothing to worry about.

But Harry wasn't worried; he was just focused on doing his best. He might only have a few weeks to impress his new coaches, so he had to get things right. If Harry missed one shot, he had to score the next one.

'How did it go?' Pat asked when he returned to pick him up.

'It was good,' was all Harry said. This time, he was taking it one step at a time. He didn't want to get carried away. It was just nice to be training with a professional team again.

But it turned out that Watford weren't the only ones chasing him. Another club was also interested, the only club in Harry's heart – Tottenham.

Tottenham's youth scout Mark O'Toole had been watching Harry's Ridgeway Rovers performances for nearly a year. Harry was easily the best player in his team. He was a natural finisher and he had good technique. So, what was Mark waiting for?

'He knows exactly where the goal is but most

strikers are either big or quick,' he discussed with the other scouts. 'Harry's neither!'

Mark liked to be 100 per cent certain before he told the Tottenham youth coaches to offer a youngster a trial. But when he heard that Harry was at Watford, he decided to take a risk, and advised the coaches:

'I want you to take a look at a kid who plays for Ridgeway Rovers. He scores lots of goals but he's not a classic striker. I guess he's more like Teddy Sheringham than Alan Shearer.'

'Interesting! What's his name?'

'Harry Kane.'

'Well, tell him to come down for a trial.'

When his dad told him the news, Harry thought his family were playing a prank on him. How could they be so mean? Surely, they knew how much he wanted to play for his local club.

'No, I'm serious!' Pat told him. He tried to look serious but he couldn't stop smiling. 'I got a call from a Tottenham youth scout. They want you to go down to the training centre next week.'

After checking a few times, Harry celebrated with a lap of the living room.

'I'm going to play for Tottenham! I'm going to play for Tottenham!'

He had only been training with Watford for about a month, but there was no way that he could say no to Spurs. His dream team was calling him.

Harry waited and worried but finally the big day arrived.

'How are you feeling?' Pat asked as they drove to Spurs Lodge in Epping Forest.

Harry nodded. His heart was beating so fast that he thought it might jump out of his mouth if he tried to speak.

'Just remember to enjoy it, son,' his dad told him. 'It's a big opportunity but you've got to have fun, okay?'

Harry nodded again. Nothing was as fun as scoring goals.

As they parked their car, Harry could see the other boys warming up on the pitch. In their matching club tracksuits, they seemed to be having a great time together. This was the Under-13s but they all looked at least fifteen. Harry was still waiting for his growth spurt. What if they didn't want a little kid to join their group? What if he made a fool of himself? No, he couldn't think like that. He had to keep believing in himself.

Mark O'Toole was there at the entrance to greet them. 'Welcome to Tottenham! Are you ready for this, kid?'

This time, Harry had to speak. 'Yes, thanks.'

After a deep breath, he walked out onto the pitch in his lucky Tottenham shirt. He had nothing to lose.

Two hours later, Harry was on his way back home, sweaty and buzzing.

'They scored first but I knew we would win it. We had all the best players. George is really good in midfield and Danny can dribble past anyone. I reckon he can kick it even harder than Charlie! The other team didn't stand a chance, really. We had to work hard but–'

'Whoa, slow down, kiddo!' his dad laughed. 'So, you had a good time out there?'

'It was so much fun! I scored the winning goal!'

'I know – it was a great strike too.'

Harry frowned. 'How do you know that?'

His dad laughed. 'I watched from the car! I didn't want to put extra pressure on you by standing there on the sidelines but I wasn't going to miss your first session. Well done, you played really well tonight.'

After six weeks on trial, Harry became a proper Spurs youth team player. It was the proudest moment of his life but he had lots of hard work ahead of him. He had been the best player at Ridgeway Rovers, but he was now just average at Tottenham. It was like starting school all over again.

Luckily, Harry was a quick and willing learner. If it meant he got to play for Spurs, he would do anything the coaches asked him to do.

'Excellent effort, Harry!' John Moncur, the head of youth development, shouted.

Harry was enjoying himself but as summer approached, he began to worry. Soon, it would be time for the end-of-season letters again. Would Spurs decide to keep him for another year? After his experience at Arsenal, he couldn't bear another rejection. The day the post arrived, Harry's hands were shaking.

'Open it!' his brother Charlie demanded impatiently.

When he tore open the envelope, Harry read the dreaded word and his heart sank: '*Unfortunately...*'. It was the release letter. He tried to hold back the tears but he couldn't. 'I don't understand – I had a good season!'

The phone rang and Pat went to answer it. Within seconds, the sadness was gone from his voice. Instead, he sounded relieved. 'Don't worry, these things happen...Yes, I'll tell him right now.'

'Panic over!' Pat called out as he returned to the living room. Harry looked up and saw a big smile on his dad's face. What was going on? 'They sent you the wrong letter by mistake. Spurs want you to stay!'

CHAPTER 10

ONE MORE YEAR

Alex Inglethorpe was Tottenham's Under-18s coach but once a week, he helped out with the Under-14s training. He liked to keep an eye on the younger age groups because the most talented boys would soon move up into his team. Ryan Mason and Andros Townsend were already making the step-up. Who would be next?

During the session, Alex offered lots of advice, especially to the team's best players. There were a couple of speedy full-backs, plus a tall centre-back and a classy playmaker in central midfield. And then there was Harry.

Harry didn't really stand out as an amazing young

footballer, but Alex loved the boy's attitude. He played with so much desire and all he wanted to do was score goals for his team. Harry understood that he wasn't as strong or quick as the other strikers, but he didn't let that stop him. He loved a challenge, and competing with Tottenham's best young players was certainly a challenge. With the pressure on, he never panicked. He just made the most of his technique and worked hard on his weaknesses.

'That's it, Harry! Shield the ball from the defender and wait until the pass is on. Lovely!'

Harry was the perfect student. After most sessions, he would stay behind for extra shooting practice. For a youth coach, that desire was a very good sign.

'Let's wait and see what happens when he grows a bit,' Alex kept telling everyone at the Tottenham academy. But they couldn't wait forever. Next year, Harry would be moving up to the Under-16s. Before then, they had to make a big decision about his future.

'Thanks for coming,' the Under-14s coach said, shaking hands with Harry's parents. 'I wanted to talk to you about your son's progress. As you know,

everyone loves Harry here at Spurs. He works so
hard and he's a pleasure to work with.'

Pat and Kim could tell that there was a 'But'
coming.

'But we're worried. He's still small for his age
and he's not a speedy little striker like Jermain
Defoe. Don't get me wrong, Harry's got a very good
understanding of the game but he needs more than
just that if he wants to play up front for Spurs.'

'Okay, so how long does he have to get better?'
Pat asked. Once they knew the timeframe, they
could make a plan.

The Under-14s coach frowned. 'Every age group
is a big new challenge and unless we see real
improvement, we don't think that Harry will make it
in the Under-16s next year.'

So, one more year. When they got home, Pat sat
Harry down in the living room and told him the
news. He could see the tears building in his son's
eyes. First Arsenal and now Tottenham…

'Don't worry, this isn't over,' Pat said, putting an
arm around Harry's shoulder. 'We just have to work

even harder to prove them wrong. We believe in you. Do you want to give up?'

Harry shook his head firmly. 'No.'

His dad smiled. 'Good, that's my boy! We'll make a plan tomorrow.'

For the next twelve months, Harry trained with Tottenham as normal, but he also did extra sessions away from the club.

'I want to help but me and you kicking a ball around in the garden won't cut it anymore,' his dad joked. 'It's time to get serious!'

At first, 'serious' just meant lots of boring running and not much actual football. Harry did short sprints until he could barely lift his legs. 'What's the point of this?' he thought to himself as he stood there panting in the rain. This wasn't the beautiful game that he loved.

'Let's have a chat,' his coach said. He could tell that Harry was hating every second of it. 'Look kid, you're never going to be a 100-metre champion but a short burst of pace can make a huge difference for a striker.'

Harry thought back to Jermain Defoe during that street game a few years earlier. He was really good at making space for the shot and his reaction speed was amazing. That was what Harry needed. If the ball dropped in the penalty area, he had to get there first. If a goalkeeper made a save, he had to win the race to the rebound.

'Brilliant, Harry!' his coach cried out a few minutes later. 'That's your best time yet!'

Soon, they moved on to ball work. Harry practised his hold-up play, his heading and, of course, his shooting. He could feel the improvement and so could Tottenham. After a few months, Harry was looking fitter and much more confident on the pitch. Most importantly, he was a better striker and he was scoring more goals.

'Congratulations, kid!' Alex told him after another brilliant performance. 'I knew you'd prove them wrong. And you're getting taller every time I see you.'

Yes, Harry was finally growing! Everything was falling into place at just the right time. Thanks to lots of extra effort, Spurs wanted him to stay. Now, Harry just needed to grow into his tall new body.

CHAPTER 11

MEXICO AND SWITZERLAND

By the time he turned fifteen, Harry had become one of Tottenham's hottest prospects. He still played a lot of games for the Under-16s but he was also getting experience at higher levels. No matter who he played against, Harry kept scoring goals.

'That kid is one of the best natural finishers I've ever seen,' Spurs coach Tim Sherwood told Alex Inglethorpe. 'Why have I never heard of him until now?'

The Under-18s coach laughed. 'He's a late developer!'

'Okay, well look after him carefully – he could be our next goal machine.'

At the start of the 2008–09 season, Jonathan Obika had been Alex's number one striker in the Spurs academy side but the team played lots of matches and it was good to have competition for places.

'Welcome to the squad!' Alex said as he gave Harry the good news. 'At first, you'll be on the bench but if you keep making the most of your opportunities, you'll force your way into the starting line-up. You deserve this.'

Harry was delighted. Not only was he moving up but he was joining a very good side. There was Steven Caulker at the back, Ryan Mason in the middle and Andros Townsend on the wing. With teammates like that, he was going to get plenty of chances to score. Harry couldn't wait.

'If I grab a few goals, I could be playing for the first team soon!' he told Charlie excitedly.

It was his older brother's job to keep his feet on the ground. 'And if you miss a few sitters, you could be playing for the Under-16s again!' Charlie teased.

Luckily, that didn't happen. Harry kept on scoring and soon he was off on an exciting international adventure.

'I'm going to Mexico!' he told his family in December. 'I made the Spurs team for the Copa Chivas.'

'Never heard of it!' Charlie replied with a smile. He was very proud of his younger brother, but it wasn't very cool to show it.

Kim was more concerned about Christmas. 'When do you leave?' she asked.

Harry shrugged; he wasn't bothered about the details. He was playing football for Tottenham; that was all he needed to know. 'In January, I think.'

It was going to be the trip of a lifetime. He couldn't wait to have lots of fun with Ryan, Steven and Andros and win the tournament. What an experience it would be!

'Just you behave yourself,' his mum told him at the airport. 'Don't let the older boys get you into trouble!'

After a long flight, the squad arrived in Guadalajara

and found the familiar Tottenham cockerel on the side of a big coach.

'We're famous!' Ryan joked as they all got on board.

In the Copa Chivas, Tottenham faced teams from Spain, Costa Rica, Brazil, Paraguay, Norway and, of course, Mexico.

'Come on boys, we're representing England here!' Harry said, looking down at their white Spurs shirts.

It was hard work in the heat but Tottenham did well. In eight matches, Harry managed to score three goals.

'Only Ryan got more than me!' he told his parents proudly when he returned to Chingford. It had been the best trip ever, but he was glad to get back to his own bedroom and home cooking.

A few months later, Harry was off again. Tottenham were playing in the *Torneo Bellinzona* in Switzerland against big clubs like Sporting Lisbon and Barcelona.

'Barca who?' Steven joked. They weren't scared of anyone.

Harry started two of their five matches and, although he didn't score, he played a big role in helping his team to win the tournament.

'I like setting up goals too, you know!' he reminded Ryan after their final win. It was a great feeling but nothing beat scoring goals.

Harry had really enjoyed his travels and he had learnt a lot from playing against teams from other countries. But back in England, it was time to think about his Spurs future. With his sixteenth birthday coming up, would Tottenham offer him a scholarship contract? He felt like he was improving all the time but he didn't want to get his hopes up. As time went by, his fears grew.

'Harry, have you got any plans for Tuesday?' John McDermott, the head of the academy, asked him casually.

He quickly worked out the date in his head. 'That's my birthday! Why?'

John smiled. 'Do you think you'll have time to come in and sign your contract?

Harry had never felt so relieved. He couldn't wait

to tell his family and friends. After all his hard work, he was finally getting his reward. Signing with Spurs would be the best birthday present ever.

CHAPTER 12

GETTING CLOSER

Ahead of the 2009–10 season, the Tottenham Under-18s lined up for their squad photo. Harry had grown so much that the cameraman placed him on the back row next to the goalkeepers. He wasn't yet important enough to sit in the front row, but that was where he aimed to be next year.

Once everyone was in position, the cameraman counted down. '3, 2, 1… Click!'

Most of his teammates looked very serious in the photos but Harry couldn't help smiling. Why shouldn't he be happy? He was playing football for his favourite club in the world!

Harry's season started in Belgium at Eurofoot.

Ryan, Andros and Steven had all gone out on loan, so he was suddenly a senior member of the youth squad.

'A lot of excellent players have played in this tournament,' coach Alex Inglethorpe told them. 'This is going to be a great experience for all of you. We will be playing a lot of games while we're out here, so get ready to test your fitness!'

After his successful trips to Mexico and Switzerland, Harry couldn't wait for his next international adventure. He was a year older now and a much better striker. The tournament schedule was really tiring but Harry scored three goals in his first four games.

'You're on fire!' his strike partner Kudus Oyenuga cheered as they celebrated their win over Dutch team Willem II.

In the end, Tottenham didn't reach the semi-finals but Harry had his shooting boots on, ready for the Premier Academy League to begin. Or so he thought, anyway. But after four matches, he still hadn't scored.

'Just be patient,' Kudus kept telling him.

It was easy for Kudus to say; he had already found the net three times. 'But scoring goals is what I do best!' Harry argued.

'I think you're just trying too hard,' Tom Carroll, their tiny midfield playmaker, suggested. 'Just relax and I bet the goals will come.'

Harry was grateful for his teammates' support and advice. He scored in his next match against Fulham and once he started, he didn't stop. After two free-kick strikes against Watford, first-team coach Harry Redknapp picked him as a sub for the League Cup match against Everton.

'No way! This is too good to be true,' Harry said when he saw the squad list. His name was there next to top professionals like Jermaine Jenas and Vedran Ćorluka.

Alex laughed. 'No, it's for real! Just don't get your hopes up; you probably won't get off the bench.'

Harry didn't come on, but he got to train with his heroes and share a dressing room with them. The experience inspired him to keep working hard. He could feel himself getting closer and closer to his Tottenham dream.

By Christmas, Harry was the Under-18s top scorer with nine goals, and the new academy captain.

'Alex always had a good feeling about you,' John McDermott said as he congratulated Harry. 'You're certainly proving him right these days! If you keep it up, the future is yours.'

Harry celebrated by scoring his first hat-trick of the season against Coventry City. And the great news just kept coming. In January 2010, he was called up to the England Under-17s for the Algarve Tournament in Portugal.

'Welcome!' the coach John Peacock said at his first squad meeting. 'I guess you must know a lot of these guys from the Premier Academy League?'

'Yes,' Harry replied, trying to hide his nerves. He had played against Benik Afobe, Ross Barkley and Nathaniel Chalobah before but they probably didn't even remember him. He was the new kid and he suddenly felt very shy. Luckily, his new teammates were very friendly.

'Nice to meet you, we needed a new striker,'
Nathaniel grinned. 'Benik already thinks he's Thierry
Henry!'

Harry soon felt like one of the gang. Off the pitch,
they had lots of fun together but on the pitch, they
were a focused team. The Under-17 European
Championships were only a few months away, and
so the Algarve Tournament was a chance for players
to secure their places.

As he walked onto the pitch wearing the Three
Lions on his shirt for the first time, Harry had to
pinch himself to check that he wasn't dreaming. A
few years earlier, Spurs had been close to letting him
go – but now look at him! It was hard to believe.
Harry didn't score against France or Ukraine but
he would never forget those matches. He was an
England youth international now.

Harry knew that if he played well until May, he
had a chance of going to the Euros in Liechtenstein.
That's what he wanted more than anything. He kept
scoring goals for the Tottenham Under-18s and the
Reserves, and crossed his fingers. He finished with

eighteen goals in only twenty-two Premier Academy League games. Surely that would be enough to make the England squad?

In the end, Harry never found out because he was too ill to go to the tournament. Instead of representing his country at the Euros, he had to sit at home and watch Nathaniel, Ross and Benik winning without him. When England beat Spain in the final, Harry was both delighted and devastated.

'Congratulations, guys!' he texted his teammates but inside, he was very jealous. He should have been there with them, lifting the trophy.

'You'll get more chances,' his mum told him as he lay on the sofa feeling sorry for himself.

It didn't seem that way at the time, but Harry always bounced back from disappointments. There was a new season to prepare for, and a first professional Tottenham contract to sign. That was more than enough to lift him out of his bad mood. It was the best feeling in the world as he signed his name on the papers.

'Thanks for always believing in me,' Harry told

Alex as they chatted afterwards. 'I couldn't have done this without you.'

His Under-18s coach shook his head. 'You did it all yourself but you haven't achieved anything yet, kid. The next step is the hardest but you've got what it takes.'

Harry smiled. It was true; he wouldn't give up until he made it into the Spurs first team.

CHAPTER 13

EXPERIENCE NEEDED

At seventeen, Harry was on his way to becoming a Spurs superstar but he still had a lot to learn. Luckily, there were plenty of teachers around him at Tottenham. In the Reserves, he often played alongside first team stars who were recovering from injuries, like David Bentley and Robbie Keane. Harry loved those matches. He was always watching and listening for new tips.

'If you need to, take a touch but if you hit it early, you might catch the keeper out.'

'Don't just assume that he's going to catch it. Get there in case he drops it!'

By 2010, Harry was also training regularly with

Harry Redknapp's squad. It was hard to believe
that he was sharing a pitch with world-class players
like Gareth Bale, Luka Modrić and Rafael van der
Vaart. But best of all, Harry was working with his
hero, Jermain Defoe. Eventually, he plucked up the
courage to talk about that street game.

'Oh yeah, I remember that!' Jermain laughed.
'That was you? Wow, I feel *really* old now!'

Jermain became Harry's mentor and invited him to
his extra shooting sessions.

'You're a natural goalscorer, H, but it takes more
than instinct to become a top striker. You need to
practise, practise, practise! What are you aiming for
when you shoot?'

It seemed like a really stupid question. 'The goal,'
he replied.

'Okay, but what part of the goal? Top corner,
bottom corner?'

'Err, I don't know, I guess I–'

Jermain interrupted Harry. 'No, no, no! You've got
to know exactly what you're aiming at, H. Before
you hit this one, I want you to picture the goal in

your head and then aim for the top right corner.'

Harry took his time and placed the ball carefully into the top right corner.

'Good, but you won't get that long to think in a real match.'

Jermain called a young defender over: 'As soon as I play the pass to Harry, close him down.'

Under pressure, Harry hit the target again but his shot went straight down the middle of the goal. 'No, the keeper would have saved that,' Jermain said. So Harry tried again and again until he hit that top right corner.

'Nice! Now let's work on making that space to shoot. Let's hope you're quicker than you look!' Jermain teased.

He was very impressed by Harry's attitude. Not only did he love scoring goals but he also loved improving his game. That was a winning combination. Jermain kept telling the Spurs coaches, 'If you give him a chance, I promise you he'll score!'

But for now, Redknapp already had Jermain, Roman Pavlyuchenko and Peter Crouch in his squad.

Harry would have to wait for his chance. He was doing well for the Reserves but was that the best place for him to develop? Spurs' youth coaches didn't think so.

'He's a great kid and a talented player but what's his best position?' Les Ferdinand asked Tim Sherwood.

That was a difficult question. Harry was a natural finisher but he was also good on the ball. He could read the game well as a second striker, linking the midfield and attack.

Sherwood's silence proved Ferdinand's point. 'That's the big issue. He's a goalscorer but he's not strong enough to battle against big centre-backs.'

'Not yet, no.'

'Plus, he's not quick enough to get in behind the defence.'

This time, Sherwood disagreed. 'He's quicker than he looks and he's lethal in the box.'

After a long discussion, the Spurs coaches agreed on an action plan – Harry would go out on loan in January 2011 to a lower league club.

'We've spoken to Leyton Orient and they want to take you for the rest of the season,' Sherwood told him in a meeting.

At first, Harry was surprised and upset. He didn't want to leave Tottenham, even if it was only for a few months.

'Look, kid, a spell in League One will be good for you,' Sherwood explained. 'You need first-team experience and you're not going to get that here at the moment, I'm afraid. We also need to toughen you up a bit, put some muscle on that skinny frame. Don't worry – we're not going to forget about you!'

Harry spoke to his parents and he spoke to his teammates. They all agreed that it was a good idea.

'Everyone goes out on loan at some point,' Ryan told him. 'It's better than being stuck in the Reserves, trust me!'

'I was at Orient last season,' Andros told him. 'It's a good club and they'll look after you. At least, Spurs aren't asking you to go miles from home. Leyton is just up the road!'

They were right, of course. If a loan move to

Leyton Orient would help him to improve and get into the Tottenham first team, Harry would go. It really helped that he wouldn't be going alone.

'Let's do this!' Tom cheered as they travelled to their first training session together.

CHAPTER 14

LEYTON ORIENT

Rochdale's pitch looked bad even before the match kicked off. Where had all the grass gone? As the Leyton Orient squad warmed up, they kept away from the boggy penalty areas and corners. They didn't want to make things worse. When Harry tried a short sprint, his boots sank into the squelch and it was difficult to lift them out. How was he supposed to make runs into the box?

Orient's striker Scott McGleish watched and laughed. 'Welcome to League One, kid!'

The Spotland Stadium was certainly no White Hart Lane. After seventy minutes of football and heavy rain, it looked more like a mud bath than a pitch. On

the bench, Harry sat with his hood up, shaking his
legs to keep warm. The score was 1–1, perfect for a
super sub...

'Harry, you're coming on!' the assistant manager
Kevin Nugent turned and shouted.

This was it – his Leyton Orient debut. Harry
jumped to his feet and took off his tracksuit. As he
waited on the touchline, he didn't even notice the
rain falling. He was so focused on making a good first
impression for his new club.

'It's fun out there today!' Scott joked, high-fiving
Harry as he left the field.

Harry grinned and ran on. He was desperate to
make a difference, either by scoring or creating the
winning goal. He chased after every ball but before
he knew it, the final whistle went.

'Well done, lad,' his manager Russell Slade said,
slapping his wet, muddy back.

Harry had enjoyed his first short battle against the
big League One centre-backs. They wanted to teach
the Premier League youngster about 'real football',
and he wanted to show them that this Premier

League youngster could cope with 'real football'.
Scott was right; it *was* fun!

'So, how did you find it?' Kevin asked back in
the dressing room. Alex Inglethorpe had left him in
charge of Harry and Tom during their loan spell at
the club.

'It's different, that's for sure!' Harry replied after a
nice hot shower. 'I need to get stronger but I'm ready
for the challenge.'

Orient's assistant manager was impressed. The kid
had a great attitude and that was very important
in professional football. He could see the hunger in
his eyes.

Harry was picked to start the next home game
against Sheffield Wednesday. It was a big responsibility
for a seventeen-year-old. He fought hard up front but
it wasn't easy against really experienced defenders. At
half-time, it was still 0–0.

'You're causing them lots of problems,' Kevin
reassured him. 'Keep doing what you're doing and
be patient.'

Harry felt more confident as he ran out for the

second half. He had fifteen, or maybe twenty, minutes to grab a goal before the manager took him off. 'I can do this,' he told himself.

When Orient took the lead, the whole team breathed a sigh of relief. They started passing the ball around nicely and creating more chances. Harry only needed one. When it arrived, he steadied himself and placed his shot carefully.

Goooooooooooooooaaaaaaaaaaaaaaaaaaalllllllllllllllllllllllll!!!!!!!!!!!!!!!!!!!!!!!

He had scored on his full debut! Harry ran towards the Orient fans to celebrate. It felt like the start of big things.

'You're one of us now!' Scott cheered as they high-fived on the touchline.

*

'So, how is Harry getting on?' Alex asked Kevin when they met up a few months later.

The Orient assistant manager chuckled. 'That boy's a real fighter, isn't he? His legs are no bigger than matchsticks but he's fearless. He's good in front of goal, too.'

'What about that red card against Huddersfield?'

Kevin shook his head. 'The second yellow was very harsh,' he explained. 'I'm not sure he even touched the guy! You know that's not Harry's way. He's one of the good guys.'

Tottenham's youth coach nodded. He knew all about Harry's character. Some youngsters really struggled to adapt to new environments, but clearly not him. Alex never had any doubt that Harry would make the most of his first-team experience.

With Orient chasing a playoff spot, Harry was back on the bench for the last few matches of the season. It wasn't where he wanted to be but he was pretty pleased with his record of five goals in eighteen games. It was a decent start to his professional career.

'Welcome back, stranger!' Ryan joked when Harry returned to Tottenham in May.

Despite going out on loan, he had never really left his beloved club. After training with Orient, Harry often went back to do extra sessions with the Spurs Under-21s. They couldn't get rid of him that easily.

Over the summer of 2011, Redknapp sold Peter

Crouch and Robbie Keane, and replaced them with Emmanuel Adebayor. Harry was feeling positive about his sums.

'Two strikers left and only one came in,' he thought to himself. 'That means one spare spot for me!'

It looked that way at the start of the 2011–12 season. In August, Harry made his Tottenham debut at White Hart Lane, against Hearts in the UEFA Europa League. They were already 5–0 up from the first leg, so Redknapp threw him straight into the starting line-up, with Andros and Tom. Harry had never been so excited.

'I'm keeping Jermain out of the team!' he joked with his brother.

'What shirt number did they give you?' Charlie asked.

'37.'

'And what number is Jermain?'

'18.'

'Well, you're not the star striker yet then, bro!'

But Harry wasn't giving up until he *was* Tottenham's star striker. In the twenty-eighth minute, he chased after Tom's brilliant through-ball. It was a move that they had practised so many times in the Spurs youth teams. Harry got there first, just ahead of the Hearts keeper, who tripped him. Penalty!

Harry picked himself up and walked over to get the ball. This was *his* penalty, a great opportunity to score on his Spurs debut. He placed it down on the spot and took a few steps back. He tried to ignore the goalkeeper bouncing on his line. He pictured the goal in his head, just like Jermain had taught him.

After a deep breath, he ran towards the ball but suddenly, doubts crept into his head. Was it a bad idea to shoot bottom left like he usually did? He paused just before he kicked it and that gave the keeper time to make the save. Harry ran in for the rebound but it was no use; he had missed the penalty.

Harry was devastated but he didn't stand there with his head in his hands. The nightmares could wait until after the match. For now, he kept hunting for his next chance to become a Tottenham hero…

CHAPTER 15

MILLWALL

'Go out there and score!' Jermain shouted as Harry ran on to replace him.

Tottenham were already 3–0 up against Shamrock Rovers. There was still time for him to grab a fourth.

Danny Rose's cross flew over Harry's head but Andros was there at the back post. As he knocked it down, Harry reacted first and shot past the defender on the line.

Goooooooooooooooooooaaaaaaaaaaaaaaaaaalllllllllllllll llllllll!!!!!!!!!!!!!!!!!!!!!!!

Harry turned away to celebrate with Andros. What a feeling! He roared up at the sky. He was a Tottenham goalscorer now, and he could put that awful penalty miss behind him.

Unfortunately, however, that was the end of Tottenham's Europa League campaign. It was a real blow for their young players because the tournament was their big chance to shine. What would happen now? There wasn't space for them in Spurs' Premier League squad, so they would either have to go back to the Reserves or out on loan again.

'Right now, I just want to play week in week out,' Harry told his dad. 'I don't care where!'

Pat smiled. 'Be careful what you wish for. You wouldn't like the cold winters in Russia!'

In the end, Harry and Ryan were sent on loan to Millwall in January 2012. The Lions were fighting to stay in the Championship and they needed goals.

'We only scored one goal in the whole of December,' Harry's new manager Kenny Jackett moaned. 'We played five matches, that's over 450 minutes of football!'

Harry's job was clear and he couldn't wait to help his new team. In his Millwall debut against Bristol City, he had a few chances to score but he couldn't get past former England goalkeeper David James.

When City won the match with a last-minute goal, Harry couldn't believe it. He trudged off the pitch with tears in his eyes.

'Hard luck, kid,' Jackett said, putting an arm around his shoulder. 'You played well. The goals will come.'

His new strike partner, Andy Keogh, gave him similar advice. 'Just forget about the misses. If you keep thinking about them, you'll never score!'

The Millwall players and coaches liked Harry and they wanted him to do well. Despite his talent, he wasn't an arrogant wonderkid who thought he was way too good for them. He was a friendly guy, who worked hard for the team and always wanted to improve.

But six weeks later, Harry was still waiting for his first league goal for Millwall. It was the longest drought of his whole life. What was going wrong? Why couldn't he just put the ball in the net? Eventually, he did it away at Burnley.

He made the perfect run and James Henry played the perfect pass. Harry was through on goal. Surely, he couldn't miss this one! The goalkeeper rushed out to stop him but he stayed calm and used his side foot to guide the ball into the bottom corner.

Gooooooooooooooooaaaaaaaaaaaaaaaaalllllllllllllllll lllllllllllll!!!!!!!!!!!!!!!!!!!

Harry pumped his fists and jumped into the air. It was finally over! James threw himself into Harry's arms.

'Thanks mate!' Millwall's new goalscorer shouted above the noise of the fans. 'There's no stopping me now!'

With his confidence back, Harry became a goal machine once more. The Championship defenders just couldn't handle his movement. He was deadly in the penalty area, hitting the target with every shot and header. But he was also brilliant when he played behind the striker. In a deeper role, he had the technique and vision to set up goals.

'Cheers!' Andy shouted after scoring from his perfect pass.

Harry also loved to hit a long-range rocket. Against Peterborough, he spun away from his marker and chased after the ball. It was bouncing high and he was on his weaker left foot, but Harry was feeling bold. Why not? Jermain and Robbie had taught him a very important lesson at Tottenham – if you shoot early, the keeper won't be ready. Harry struck his shot powerfully and accurately into the far corner.

Goooooooooooooooooooooaaaaaaaaaaaaaaaaaallllllllllllllllllllllllll!!!!!!!!!!!!!!

Harry ran towards the fans and slid across the grass on his knees.

'You're on fire!' Andy cheered as they celebrated together.

With his nine goals, Harry won Millwall's Young Player of the Season award. It was a proud moment for him and a nice way to say goodbye to the club.

'We're going to miss you!' Jackett told him after his last training session. 'It's been a pleasure working with you. Good luck back at Spurs – you're going to be great.'

Harry was sad to leave Millwall but he was also excited about returning to Tottenham. He had learnt a lot from his loan experience. He was now a stronger player, both physically and mentally. It was much harder to push him off the ball, and much harder to stop him scoring.

'2012–13 is going to be my season!' Harry told his family confidently.

But first, he was off to play for England at the UEFA European Under-19 Championships in Estonia. Nathaniel, Benik and Ross were in the squad too, along with some exciting new players: Eric Dier was a tough defender and Nathan Redmond was a tricky winger.

'There's no reason why we can't win this!' their manager Noel Blake told them.

Although he wore the Number 10 shirt, Harry played in midfield behind Benik and Nathan. He enjoyed his playmaker role but it made it harder for him to do his favourite thing – scoring goals. After a draw against Croatia and a win over Serbia, England needed to beat France to reach the semi-finals.

As the corner came in, most of the England attackers charged towards the goal. But not Harry. He waited around the penalty spot because he had noticed that the French goalkeeper wasn't very good at catching crosses. When he fumbled the ball, it fell straight to Harry, who was totally unmarked. He calmly volleyed it into the net.

Goooooooooooooooooooooaaaaaaaaaaaaaaaalllllllllllll lllllllllllllll!!!!!!!!!!!!!!!!!!!!!!

2–1 to England! Harry pumped his fists and pointed up at the sky. He was delighted to score such an important goal for his country.

'You're a genius!' Eric cheered as the whole team celebrated.

Unfortunately, Harry wasn't there to be England's hero in the semi-final against Greece. He had to watch from the bench as his teammates lost in extra-time. It was such a horrible way to crash out of the tournament.

'At least we've got the Under-20 World Cup next summer!' Harry said, trying to make everyone feel a little bit better.

He focused once again on his top target – breaking into the Tottenham first team.

CHAPTER 16

TOUGH TIMES

On the opening day of the 2013–14 season, Harry travelled up to Newcastle with the Tottenham squad. New manager André Villas-Boas wanted to give his young players a chance. Jake Livermore started the match, and Harry and Andros waited impatiently on the subs bench. Would this be the day when they made their Premier League debuts?

'Is it bad to hope that someone gets injured?' Andros joked.

With ten minutes to go, Newcastle scored a penalty to make it 2–1. Harry's heart was racing; surely, this was going to be his moment. Tottenham needed to score again and he was the only striker on the bench.

'Harry, you're coming on!'

He quickly took off his yellow bib, and then his grey tracksuit. He pulled up his socks and re-laced his boots. He tucked his navy-blue Spurs shirt into his white shorts. '37 KANE' was ready for action.

'Good luck!' Andros said as Harry walked down to the touchline.

'Get a goal!' Villas-Boas said as Harry waited to come on.

'Let's do this!' Jermain cheered as Harry ran on to join him up front.

Harry had less than ten minutes to score and become an instant Spurs hero. Anything was possible but Newcastle were in control of the game. Harry's Premier League debut was over before he'd really touched the ball.

'Don't worry, that was just a first taste of the action,' Jermain promised him.

Harry hoped that his mentor was right. He shook hands with his opponents and the match officials. Then he walked over to clap the Tottenham fans in the away stand. He had done his best to save the day for his club.

He couldn't wait for his next chance to play but he wasn't even a substitute for their next match against West Brom. With Emmanuel Adebayor back in the team, he was back in the Reserves. Harry was disappointed but he didn't give up.

'I'm still only nineteen,' he told himself. 'I've got plenty of time to shine.'

A few days later, he joined Norwich City on loan for the rest of the season. The Canaries were in the Premier League, so this was a great opportunity to show Spurs that he was good enough to play at the top level.

'Bring it on!' he told his new manager Chris Hughton.

Against West Ham, Harry came on with twenty minutes to go. That gave him plenty of time to score. He dribbled forward, cut inside and curled the ball just wide of the post.

'So close!' Harry groaned, putting his hands on his head.

Minutes later, he beat the West Ham right-back and pulled the ball back to Robert Snodgrass… but his shot was blocked on the line! Somehow, the match finished 0–0 but Harry was happy with his debut.

Afterwards, Hughton told the media, 'I think Kane will be a super player'.

Harry was delighted with the praise. His first start for Norwich soon arrived against Doncaster in the League Cup. He couldn't wait.

'I'm definitely going to score!' he told his teammates.

Sadly, Harry didn't score and he only lasted fifty minutes. He tried to carry on but he couldn't; his foot was way too painful. He winced and limped off the pitch.

'What happened?' his brother asked as he rested on the sofa back at home.

'I've fractured a metatarsal,' Harry explained.

'Isn't that what Becks did before the 2002 World Cup?' Charlie joked, trying to cheer his brother up. 'You've got to stop copying him!'

Harry smiled, but he was dreading the surgery and then the months without football. It would drive him crazy.

'You're a strong character,' Alex Inglethorpe told him when he returned to Tottenham, 'and you're going to come back even stronger!'

Harry's new girlfriend helped to take his mind off his injury. He and Katie had gone to the same primary and secondary schools but it was only later that they started dating. They got on really well and made each other laugh, even during the tough times.

Harry spent October and November in the gym, slowly getting his foot ready to play football again. It was long, boring work but he had to do it if he wanted to be playing again before the new year. That was his big aim. In December, Harry started training with the first team again, and starring for the Reserves.

'I'm feeling good!' Harry told his manager Chris Hughton with a big smile on his face. It was great to be playing football again. He had missed it so much.

On 29 December 2012, he was a sub for the

Manchester City match. By half-time, Norwich were losing 2–1.

'They're down to ten men, so let's get forward and attack,' Hughton told his players in the dressing room. 'We can win this! Harry, you're coming on to replace Steve.'

Harry's eyes lit up. He had been hoping for ten, maybe fifteen, minutes at the end but instead he was going to play the whole second half.

This was his biggest challenge yet. Harry was up against City's captain Vincent Kompany, one of the best centre-backs in the world. These were the big battles that he dreamed about. Harry held the ball up well and made clever runs into space. He didn't score but he was back in business.

'Boss, that was just the start!' he promised Hughton.

Before long, however, Harry was told that he had to return to Tottenham. Villas-Boas wanted a third striker as back-up for Jermain and Emmanuel. Harry was happy to help his club but he wanted to play regular football. What was the point of him being there if he wasn't even getting on the bench? A few weeks later, Villas-Boas sent him back out on loan to Leicester City.

'This is all so confusing!' Harry moaned to Katie. It had turned into a very topsy-turvy season. 'Do Spurs want me or not?'

It was a question that no-one could answer. Harry tried his best to adapt to another new club but soon after scoring on his home debut against Blackburn, he was dropped from the Leicester starting line-up. It was a massive disappointment. It felt like his career was going backwards.

'If I'm only a sub in the Championship, how am I ever going to make it at Spurs?' he complained to his dad on the phone. Leicester felt like a very long way away from Chingford.

Pat had seen his son looking this sad before. 'Remember when you were fourteen and Tottenham told you that you weren't good enough?' he reminded him. 'You didn't give up back then and you're not going to give up now!'

Harry nodded. He *was* good enough! All he

needed was a run of games and a chance to get back into goalscoring form. He just had to believe that the breakthrough would come.

CHAPTER 17

BREAKTHROUGH

'I'm not going anywhere this season,' Harry told
Tottenham firmly. After four loan spells, he was
determined to stay at the club. 'I'm going to prove
that I should be playing here week in, week out!'

Harry wasn't a raw, skinny teenager anymore.
He was now twenty years old and he looked like a
fit, powerful striker at last. That was thanks to his
Football League experience and lots of hard work in
the gym to build up his strength. He now had even
more power in his shot.

'Looking good, H!' Jermain said in pre-season
training. His encouragement was working. Harry was
getting better and better.

The 2013 U-20 World Cup in Turkey had been
a very disappointing tournament for England, but
not for Harry. He set up their first goal against
Iraq with a brilliant header, and a few days later
scored a great equaliser against Chile from outside
the penalty area. He hit the ball perfectly into the
bottom corner, just like he did again and again on
the training ground.

'What a strike!' England teammate Ross Barkley
said to Harry as they high-fived.

When he returned to England in July, Harry felt
ready to become a Premier League star but again,
Spurs had signed a new striker. Roberto Soldado
cost £26 million after scoring lots of goals for
Valencia in La Liga. Watching his rival in action,
Harry didn't give up. He believed in himself more
than ever.

For now, cup matches were Harry's chance to
shine. In the fourth round of the League Cup, Spurs
were heading for a disastrous defeat as opponents
Hull took the lead in extra-time. Could Harry save
the day?

When Jermain passed the ball to him, he had his back to goal, and needed to turn as quickly as possible. Harry used his strength and speed to spin cleverly past his marker. With a second touch, he dribbled towards the penalty area. He was in shooting range now. There were defenders right in front of him, blocking the goal, but he knew exactly where the bottom corner was. Harry could picture it in his head.

Goooooooooooooooooooooaaaaaaaaaaaaaaaalllllllllll lllllllllllllll!!!!!!!!!!!!!!

Yes! Harry pumped his fists and ran towards the fans. The job wasn't done yet but his strike had put Spurs back in the game. When the tie went to penalties, he was one of the first to volunteer.

'I've got this,' he told Spurs manager André Villas-Boas. It was time to make up for that miss in the Europa League.

Harry was Spurs' fifth penalty taker. The pressure was on – he had to score, otherwise they were out of the competition. This time, he felt confident. He had a plan and he was going to stick to it, no matter

what. As the goalkeeper dived to the right, Harry
slammed his shot straight down the middle. The net
bulged – what a relief!

'Well done, you showed a lot of guts there,' Tim
Sherwood told him afterwards, giving him a hug.
'Your time is coming!'

In December 2013, Sherwood took over as
Tottenham manager for the rest of the season,
after the sacking of Villas-Boas. Harry didn't want
to get his hopes up but he knew that his former
Under-21 coach believed in his talent. Hopefully,
Sherwood would give him more opportunities now.
By February, he was coming off the bench more
regularly but only because Jermain had signed for
Toronto FC in Canada.

'I can't believe you're leaving!' Harry told him as
they said goodbye. It was one of his saddest days at
White Hart Lane. 'It won't be the same around here
without you.'

Jermain smiled. 'It's time for me to move on and
it's time for you to step up. I want you to wear this
next season.'

It was Jermain's Number 18 shirt. Harry couldn't believe it.

'Wow, are you sure?' he asked. It would be such an honour to follow in his hero's footsteps. 'I promise to do you proud!'

Harry did just that when he finally got his first Premier League start for Tottenham against Sunderland in April. After years of waiting, Harry's time had come. He had never been so nervous in his life.

'Relax, just do what you do best,' Sherwood told him before kick-off. He was showing lots of faith in his young striker. 'Score!'

In the second half, Christian Eriksen curled a beautiful cross into the six-yard box. As the ball bounced, Harry made a late run and snuck in ahead of the centre-back to steer the ball into the bottom corner.

Goooooooooooooooooooaaaaaaaaaaaaaallllllllllllllll llllllllllll!!!!!!!!!!!!!!!!!!

Harry was buzzing. With his arms out wide like an aeroplane, he ran towards the Spurs fans near the corner flag. He had scored his first Premier League goal for Tottenham. It was time to celebrate in style.

Aaron Lennon chased after him and jumped up on his back. 'Yes, mate, what a goal!' he cheered.

Harry was soon in the middle of a big player hug. He was part of the team now and that was the greatest feeling ever.

There were six more league matches in the season and Harry started all of them. He was full of confidence and full of goals. Against West Bromwich, Aaron dribbled down the right wing and crossed into the six-yard box. Harry jumped highest and headed the ball past the defender on the line.

Goooooooooooooooooooaaaaaaaaaaaaaaaaalllllllllllll llllllllllllllll!!!!!!!!!!!!!!!!!!

A week later, they did it again. Aaron crossed the ball and Harry flicked it in. 2–1 to Tottenham!

'You've scored in three games in a row,' Emmanuel Adebayor shouted over the White Hart Lane noise. 'You're a goal machine!'

Harry had also already become a favourite with

the fans. They loved nothing more than cheering for their local hero.

He's one of our own,
He's one of our own,
Harry Kane – he's one of our own!

Even an own goal against West Ham didn't stop Harry's rise. In only six weeks, he had gone from sub to England's hottest new striker.

'What an end to the season!' Tim Sherwood said as they walked off the pitch together. 'You'll be playing for a different manager next season, but don't worry. If you keep banging in the goals, you're going to be a Tottenham hero, no matter what!'

CHAPTER 18

EXCITING TIMES AT TOTTENHAM

'Do you think he'll bring in a big new striker?' Harry asked Andros during preseason.

His friend and teammate just shrugged. They would have to wait and see what the new Tottenham manager, Mauricio Pochettino, would do.

As the 2014–15 season kicked off, Spurs had signed a new goalkeeper, some new defenders and a new midfielder. But no new striker! That left only Emmanuel, Roberto and Harry. Harry was feeling really good about his chances. He worked extra hard to impress Pochettino.

'Great work, you've certainly got the desire that I'm looking for in my players,' his manager told him.

'This could be a huge season for you!'

Emmanuel started up front against West Ham in the Premier League but it was Harry, not Roberto, who came on for the last ten minutes. That was a good sign. If he kept scoring goals in other competitions, surely Pochettino would have no choice but to let him play. Harry got five goals in the Europa League and three in the League Cup.

'Kane needs to start in the Premier League!' the fans shouted in the stands.

Harry was making a name for himself with the England Under-21s too. He loved representing his country, especially in the big games. Against France, he positioned himself between the two centre-backs and waited like a predator. When Tom Ince played the through-ball, Harry was already on the move, chasing after it. He was too smart for the French defenders and he chipped his shot over the diving goalkeeper.

Goooooooooooooooooooaaaaaaaaaaaaaaaaaaaallllllllll llllllllllllll!!!!!!!!!!!!!!!

Two minutes later, Tom crossed from the right and

Harry was there in the six-yard box to tap the ball into the net.

'That's a proper striker's goal!' his teammate told him as they celebrated together.

Tom was right. Harry was a real goalscorer now, always in the right place at the right time. 'That's thirteen goals in twelve games!' he replied proudly.

By November 2014, there was lots of pressure on Pochettino to give Harry more game-time in the Premier League. Away at Aston Villa, he came on for Emmanuel with half an hour to go.

'Come on, we can still win this match!' his old friend Ryan Mason told him. Soon, Andros was on the pitch too. They were all living their Spurs dreams together.

In injury time, Tottenham won a free kick just outside the penalty area. It was Harry's last chance to save the day for Spurs. Érik Lamela wanted to take it but Harry wasn't letting his big opportunity go. He took a long, deep breath to calm his beating heart. He looked down at the ball and then up at the goal. 'This is going in!' he told himself.

He pumped his legs hard as he ran towards the ball. He needed as much power as possible. But rather than kicking it with the top of his boot, he kicked it with the side. As the ball swerved through the air, it deflected off the head of a Villa defender and past their scrambling keeper.

Goooooooooooooooaaaaaaaaaaaaaaaaaalllllllllllllllll llllllllll!!!!!!!!!!!!!!!!!!!

It was the biggest goal that Harry had ever scored. He ran screaming towards the corner flag with all of his teammates behind him. In all the excitement, Harry threw himself down onto the grass for his favourite childhood celebration – the Klinsmann dive. Soon, he was at the bottom of a pile of happy players.

'What a beauty!' Danny Rose cheered in his face.

After scoring the match-winner, Harry was the talk of Tottenham. The fans had a new local hero and they wanted him to play every minute of every game. Against Hull City, Christian Eriksen's free kick hit the post but who was there to score the rebound? Harry!

Even when he didn't score for a few matches, Pochettino stuck with Harry. As a young player, he was still learning about playing at the top level.

'I believe in you,' his manager told him. 'You've got lots of potential and you've got the hunger to improve.'

With Pochettino's support, Harry bounced back against Swansea City. As Christian whipped in the corner kick, Harry made a late run into the box. He leapt high above his marker and powered his header down into the bottom corner.

Goooooooooooooooooooooaaaaaaaaaaaaallllllllllllllll llllllllll!!!!!!!!!!!!!!!!!

Once he started scoring, Harry couldn't stop. He was such a natural finisher. On Boxing Day, Harry even scored against one of his old teams. Only eighteen months earlier, he had been sitting on the Leicester City bench. Now, he was causing them all kinds of problems as Tottenham's star striker. With hard work and great support, he was proving everyone wrong yet again.

Pochettino was delighted with his young striker's

form but he didn't want him to burn out. 'Get some rest because we've got big games coming up.'

Harry was so excited about the 2015 fixture list ahead – Chelsea on New Year's Day and then a few weeks later, the biggest game of them all: The North London Derby – Tottenham vs Arsenal.

'Don't worry, boss,' he said with a big smile. 'I'll be ready to score some more!'

CHAPTER 19

GOALS, GOALS AND MORE GOALS

As the Tottenham team walked out of the tunnel
at White Hart Lane, Harry was second in line, right
behind their goalkeeper and captain, Hugo Lloris. He
had come so far in the last eighteen months – it was
still hard to believe. There were thousands of fans
in the stadium, cheering loudly for their team, and
cheering loudly for him.

He's one of our own,
He's one of our own,
Harry Kane – he's one of our own!

Harry looked down at the young mascot who was

holding his hand. Ten years before, that had been one of his biggest dreams – to walk out on to the pitch with his Spurs heroes. Now, he was the Spurs hero, so what was his new dream? Goals, goals and more goals, starting against their London rivals Chelsea.

'Come on, we can't let them beat us again!' Harry shouted to Ryan and Andros. They were all fired up and ready to win.

Chelsea took the lead, but Harry didn't let his head drop. It just made him even more determined to score. He got the ball on the left wing and dribbled infield. He beat one player and then shrugged off another. He only had one thing on his mind – goals. When he was just outside the penalty area, he looked up.

He was still a long way out and there were lots of Chelsea players in his way, but Harry could shoot from anywhere. The Premier League would soon know just how lethal he was. For now, however, the defenders gave him just enough space. His low, powerful strike skidded across the wet grass, past the keeper and right into the bottom corner.

Goooooooooooooooaaaaaaaaaaaaaaaalllllllllllllllllllll llllll!!!!!!!!!!!!!!!!!!!!!!

Game on! Harry ran towards the Tottenham fans and jumped into the air. He was used to scoring goals now, but this was one of his best and most important.

'You could outshoot a cowboy!' Kyle Walker joked as he climbed up on Harry's back.

At half-time, Spurs were winning 3–1 but Harry wanted more. 'We're not safe yet,' he warned his teammates. 'We've got to keep going!'

As the pass came towards him, Harry was just inside the Chelsea box with his back to goal. It didn't look dangerous at first but one lovely touch and spin later, it was very dangerous indeed. Harry stayed calm and placed his shot past the goalkeeper. It was like he'd been scoring top goals for years.

'Kane, that's gorgeous!' the TV commentator shouted. 'How good is *he*?'

The answer was: unstoppable. Even one of the best defences in the world couldn't handle him.

The match finished 5–3. It was a famous victory for Tottenham and Harry was their hero. After shaking hands with the Chelsea players, he walked around the pitch, clapping the supporters. Harry loved making them happy.

'If we play like that against Arsenal, we'll win that too!' he told Andros.

Harry got ready for the big North London Derby by scoring goals, goals and more goals. The timing was perfect; he was in the best form of his life just as Arsenal were coming to White Hart Lane. Revenge would be so sweet for Harry. Arsenal would soon realise their big mistake in letting him go.

After five minutes, Harry cut in from the left and curled a brilliant shot towards goal. He got ready to celebrate because the ball was heading for the bottom corner yet again. But the Arsenal keeper made a great save to tip it just round the post. So close! Harry put his hands to his head for a second but then kept going. If at first you don't score, shoot, shoot again.

At half-time, Tottenham were losing 1–0. 'We're

still in this game,' Pochettino told his players in the dressing room. 'If we keep creating chances, we'll score!'

When Érik took the corner, Harry stood lurking near the back post. He was waiting for the rebound. The keeper saved Mousa Dembélé's header but the ball bounced down in the box. Before the Arsenal defenders could react, Harry pounced to sweep it into the net.

Goooooooooooooooooooaaaaaaaaaaaaaaaallllllllllllllll lllllllllll!!!!!!!!!!!!!!!!!!!

Harry roared and pumped his fists. Scoring for Spurs against Arsenal meant the world to him. He had dreamed about it ever since his first trip to White Hart Lane.

'Right, let's go and win this now!' Harry told his teammates.

With five minutes to go, it looked like it was going to be a draw. As Nabil Benteleb's cross drifted into the box, Harry's eyes never left the ball. He took a couple of steps backwards and then leapt high above Laurent Koscielny. It was a very difficult chance. To score, his header would have to be really powerful and really accurate.

As soon as the ball left his head, Harry knew that he had got the angle right. It was looping towards the corner but would the keeper have time to stop it? No, Harry's perfect technique gave David Ospina no chance.

Gooooooooooooooooaaaaaaaaaaaaaaaaaalllllllllllllllll llllll!!!!!!!!!!!!!!!!!!!!

As the ball landed in the net, Harry turned away to celebrate. What a moment! With the adrenaline flooding through his veins, he slid across the grass, screaming. As he looked up, he could see the Spurs fans going crazy in the crowd. All that joy was because of him!

The final minutes felt like hours but eventually, the referee blew the final whistle. Tottenham 2, Arsenal 1! The party went on and on, both down on the pitch and up in the stands.

'I might as well retire now!' Harry joked with Ryan. 'Nothing will ever beat scoring the winner in the North London Derby.'

'Not even playing for England?' his teammate asked him. 'Mate, Roy Hodgson would be a fool not to call you up to the squad!'

Harry was desperate to play for his country. Like his hero Becks, he wanted to be the national captain one day. After doing well for the Under-21s, he was now ready to step up into the senior team. He had won both the January and February Premier League Player of the Month awards. Then, in March, Harry got the call he had been waiting for.

'I'm in!' he told his partner Katie excitedly. He wanted to tell the whole world.

'In what?' she asked. 'What are you talking about?'

'The England squad!'

The amazing news spread throughout his family. Everyone wanted a ticket to watch his international debut.

'I might not even play!' Harry warned them, but they didn't care.

He was glad to see that lots of his Tottenham teammates were in the England team too. Training with superstars like Wayne Rooney and Gary Cahill would be a lot less scary with Kyle, Andros and Danny by his side. A week later, Ryan also joined the Spurs gang.

'Thank goodness Fabian Delph got injured!' he laughed. 'I was gutted to be the only one left behind.'

They were all named as substitutes for the Euro 2016 qualifier against Lithuania at Wembley. But would any of them get to come on and play? They all sat there on the England bench, crossing their fingers and shaking with nerves.

With seventy minutes gone, England were winning 3–0. It was time for Roy Hodgson to give his young players a chance. Harry's England youth teammate Ross Barkley was the first substitute and Harry himself was the second. He was replacing Wayne Rooney.

'Good luck!' Ryan and Andros said, patting him on the back.

Harry tried to forget that he was making his England debut at Wembley. That was something he could enjoy later when the match was over. For now, he just wanted to score.

As Raheem Sterling dribbled down the left wing, Harry took up his favourite striking position near the back post. Raheem's cross came straight towards him; he couldn't miss. Harry had all the time in the world to place his header past the keeper.

Goooooooooooooooooaaaaaaaaaaaaaaaaallllllllllllllllll lllllllllllll!!!!!!!!!!!!!!!

In his excitement, Harry bumped straight into the assistant referee. 'Sorry!' he called over his shoulder as he ran towards the corner flag.

'Was that your first touch?' Danny Welbeck asked as they celebrated.

'No, it was my third or fourth,' Harry replied with a cheeky grin. 'But I've only been on the field for about a minute!'

There had been so many highlights for Harry during the 2014–15 season already, but this was the best of all. He had scored for England on his debut. All of his dedication had paid off and he felt so proud of his achievements. Harry's childhood dream had come true.

CHAPTER 20

HARRY AND DELE

'So, do you think you can score as many this season?'
Charlie asked his brother.

Lots of people thought Harry's twenty-one Premier
League goals were a one-off, a fluke. They argued
that the PFA Young Player of the Year wouldn't be as
good in 2015–16 because defenders would know all
about him now. They would mark him out of
the game.

But Harry knew that wasn't true. 'Of course I can.
In fact, I'm aiming for even more this time!'

Charlie smiled. 'Good, because when you scored
those goals against Arsenal, the guys in the pub

bought me drinks all night. Sometimes, it's fun being your brother!'

Harry was still getting used to his fame. It was crazy! Every time he took his Labradors Brady and Wilson out for a walk, there were cameras waiting for him. They even took photos of Katie when she went out shopping.

'Our normal life is over!' she complained as she flicked through the newspapers.

After a very disappointing Euro 2015 with the England Under-21s, Harry was really looking forward to the new season. It would be his first as Tottenham's top striker. With Emmanuel gone, Harry now wore the famous Number 10 shirt. He was following in the footsteps of Spurs legends Jimmy Greaves, Gary Lineker and Harry's own hero, Teddy Sheringham.

Pochettino had strengthened the Spurs squad over the summer. They had signed Son Heung-min, a goal-scoring winger, and Dele Alli, a young attacking midfielder.

Harry and Dele clicked straight away. After a few

training sessions, Dele knew where Harry would run, and Harry knew where to make space for Dele. It was like they had been playing together for years. Soon, they were making up cool goal celebrations.

'It's like you guys are back in the school playground!' captain Hugo Lloris teased, but it was great to see them getting along so well.

Despite all of his excitement, Harry didn't score a single goal in August 2015. The newspapers kept calling him a 'one-season wonder' but that only made him more determined to prove them wrong.

'You're playing well and working hard for the team,' Pochettino reassured him. 'As soon as you get one goal, you'll get your confidence back.'

Against Manchester City, Christian's brilliant free kick bounced back off the post and landed right at Harry's feet. He was in lots of space and the goalkeeper was lying on the ground. Surely he couldn't miss an open goal? Some strikers might have passed the ball carefully into the net to make sure but instead, Harry curled it into the top corner.

Goooooooooooooooooaaaaaaaaaaaaaaaaallllllllllllllllll llllllll!!!!!!!!!!!!!!!!!!!

Harry was delighted to score but most of all, he was relieved. His goal drought was over. Now, his season could really get started.

'Phew, I thought you were going to blaze that one over the bar!' Dele joked.

After that, Harry and Dele became the Premier League's deadliest double act. Between them, they had power, skill, pace and incredible shooting. By the end of February 2016, Tottenham were only two points behind Leicester City at the top of the table.

'If we keep playing like this, we'll be champions!' Pochettino told his players.

Every single one of them believed it. Spurs had the best defence in the league and were also one of the best attacking sides. Dele, Érik and Christian created lots of chances, and Harry scored lots of goals. It was one big, happy team effort. The pranks and teasing never stopped.

'How long do you have to wear that thing for?'

Dele asked during training one day. 'Halloween was months ago, you know!'

'Very funny,' Harry replied, giving his teammate a friendly punch. He was wearing a plastic face mask to protect his broken nose. 'Who knows, maybe it will bring me luck and I'll wear it forever!'

'Let's hope not!' Christian laughed.

Next up was the game that Harry had been waiting months for – the North London Derby. Could they win it again? Arsenal were only three points behind Spurs, so the match was even more important than usual.

'Come on lads, we've got to win this!' Harry shouted in the dressing room before kick-off, and all of his teammates cheered.

The atmosphere at White Hart Lane was incredible. The fans never stopped singing, even when Tottenham went 1–0 down. They believed that their team would bounce back, especially with Harry up front.

Early in the second half, Harry thought he had scored the equaliser. The goalkeeper saved his vicious shot, but surely he was behind the goal-line?

'That's in!' Harry screamed to the referee. But the technology showed that a tiny part of the ball hadn't crossed the line.

It was very frustrating but there was no point in complaining. Harry would just have to keep shooting until he got the whole ball into the net.

In the end, it was Toby Alderweireld who made it 1–1. Tottenham were playing well, but they needed a second goal to take the lead.

The ball was heading out for an Arsenal goal-kick but Dele managed to reach it and flick it back to his best friend, Harry. It looked like an impossible angle but with the supporters cheering him on, anything seemed possible. In a flash, Harry curled the ball up over the keeper and into the far corner.

Gooooooooooooooooooooaaaaaaaaaaaaaaaaaaaaaallll lllllllllllllllllll!!!!!!!!!!!!!!

It was one of the best goals Harry had ever scored. He felt on top of the world. He took off his mask as he ran and slid across the grass. Dele was right behind him and gave him a big hug.

'Maybe you *should* keep wearing that!' he joked.

Tottenham couldn't quite hold on for another big victory. A draw wasn't the result that Spurs wanted, but Harry would never forget his incredible goal.

'We're still in this title race,' Pochettino urged his disappointed players. 'We just have to win every match until the end of the season.'

Harry and Dele did their best to make their Premier League dream come true. Dele set up both of Harry's goals against Aston Villa and they scored two each against Stoke City. But with three games of the season to go, Tottenham were seven points behind Leicester.

'If we don't beat Chelsea, our season's over,' Harry warned his teammates.

At half-time, it was all going according to plan. Harry scored the first goal and Son made it 2–0. They were cruising to victory but in the second half, they fell apart. All season, the Spurs players had stayed cool and focused but suddenly, they got angry and made silly mistakes. It finished 2–2.

'We threw it away!' Harry groaned as he walked

off the pitch. He was absolutely devastated. They had worked so hard all season. And for what?

'We've learnt a lot this year,' Pochettino told his players once everyone had calmed down. 'I know you feel awful right now but you should be so proud of yourselves. Next season, we'll come back stronger and win the league!'

There was one bit of good news that made Harry feel a little better. With twenty-five goals, he had won the Premier League Golden Boot, beating Sergio Agüero and Jamie Vardy.

'And they said I was a one-season wonder!' Harry told his brother Charlie as they played golf together. A smile spread slowly across his face. He loved proving people wrong.

CHAPTER 21

ENGLAND

When Harry first joined the England squad back
in 2015, he was really nervous. It was a massive
honour to represent his country but there was a lot
of pressure too. If he didn't play well, there were lots
of other great players that could take his place. Plus,
it was scary being the new kid.

'You'll get used to this,' Wayne Rooney reassured
him. 'I remember when I first got the call-up. I was
only seventeen and it was terrifying! Just try to
ignore the talk and enjoy yourself.'

Wayne helped Harry to feel more relaxed around
the other senior players. They had fun playing golf
and table tennis together. They were nice guys and
Harry soon felt like one of the lads.

'France, here we come!' he cheered happily.

England qualified for Euro 2016 with ten wins out of ten. Harry added to his debut goal with a cheeky chip against San Marino and a low strike against Switzerland.

'At this rate, you're going to take my place in the team!' Wayne told him.

Harry shook his head. 'No, we'll play together up front!'

When Roy Hodgson announced his England squad for Euro 2016, Harry's name was there. He was delighted. There were four other strikers – Wayne, Jamie Vardy, Daniel Sturridge and Marcus Rashford – but none of them were scoring as many goals as him.

'You'll definitely play,' his brother Charlie told him.

Harry couldn't wait for his first major international tournament. His body felt pretty tired after a long Premier League season with Tottenham, but nothing was going to stop him.

'I really think we've got a good chance of winning it,' he told Dele, who was in the squad for France too.

His friend was feeling just as confident. 'If we play like we do for Spurs, we can definitely go all the way!'

Harry and Dele were both in the starting line-up for England's first group match against Russia. With Wayne now playing in midfield, Harry was England's number-one striker. He carried the country's great expectations in his shooting boots.

'I *have* to score!' he told himself as the match kicked off in Marseille.

England dominated the game but after seventy minutes, it was still 0–0. Harry got more and more frustrated. He was struggling to find the burst of pace that got him past Premier League defences. What was going wrong? His legs felt heavy and clumsy.

'Just be patient,' Wayne told him. 'If you keep getting into the right areas, the goal will come.'

When they won a free kick on the edge of the Russia box, Harry stood over the ball with Wayne and his Tottenham teammate Eric Dier. Everyone expected Harry to take it but as he ran up, he dummied the ball. Eric stepped up instead and curled the ball into the top corner. 1–0!

'Thanks for letting me take it,' he said to Harry as they celebrated the goal.

'No problem!' he replied. England had the lead and that was all that mattered.

But just as they were heading for a winning start to the tournament, Russia scored a late header. As he watched the ball flying towards the top corner, Harry's heart sank. He was very disappointed with the result and with his own performance in particular. It wasn't good enough. If he didn't improve, he would lose his place to Jamie or Daniel or Marcus.

'I believe in you, we all believe in you,' Hodgson told him after the game. 'So, believe in *yourself*!'

Harry tried not to read the player ratings in the English newspapers. Instead, he focused on bouncing back. If he could score a goal against Wales in the next game that would make everything better again.

But at half-time, it was looking like another bad day for Harry and England. He worked hard for the team but his goal-scoring touch was gone. The ball just wouldn't go in. When Gareth Bale scored a free kick to put Wales 1–0 up, Harry feared the worst.

'We need a quick goal in the second half,'
Hodgson told the team in the dressing room. 'Jamie
and Daniel, you'll be coming on to replace Harry and
Raheem.'

Harry stared down at the floor. Was that the end
of his tournament? He was really upset but he had to
accept the manager's decision.

Harry watched the second half from the bench
and cheered on his teammates. He was a good team
player. When Jamie scored the equaliser, he joined in
the celebrations. When Daniel scored the winner in
injury time, he sprinted to the corner flag to jump
on him.

'Get in!' he screamed.

It was only after the final whistle that Harry started
worrying again. Had he lost his place in the team, or
would he get another chance against Slovakia?

'I'm sorry but I've got to start Daniel and Jamie in
the next match,' Hodgson told him. 'Rest up and get
ready for the next round. We need you back, firing!'

Without Harry, England couldn't find a goal, but
0–0 was enough to take them through to the Round

of 16. He would get one more opportunity to score against Iceland, and he was pumped up for the biggest game of his international career.

It started brilliantly. Raheem was fouled in the box and Wayne scored the penalty. 1–0! It was a huge relief to get an early goal but two minutes later, it was 1–1.

'Come on, focus!' Joe Hart shouted at his teammates.

Harry and Dele both hit powerful long-range strikes that fizzed just over the crossbar. England looked in control of the game, but then Iceland scored again.

'No!' Harry shouted. His dream tournament was turning into an absolute nightmare.

England needed a hero, and quickly. Daniel crossed the ball to Harry in his favourite position near the back post. It was too low for a header so he went for the volley. Harry watched the ball carefully onto his foot and struck it beautifully. Unfortunately, it just wasn't his day, or his tournament. The goalkeeper jumped up high to make a good save. So close! Harry put his hands to his face – he was so desperate to score.

As the minutes ticked by, England started panicking. Harry's free kick flew miles wide. What a disaster! The boos from the fans grew louder.

'Stay calm, we've got plenty of time!' Hodgson called out from the touchline.

That time, however, ran out. At the final whistle, the Iceland players celebrated and the England players sank to their knees. They were out of the Euros after a terrible, embarrassing defeat.

As he trudged off the pitch, Harry was in shock. It was the worst feeling ever. He felt like he had really let his country down. Would they ever forgive him?

To take his mind off the disappointment, Harry watched American Football and focused on his future goals. With Tottenham, he would be playing in the Champions League for the first time, and trying to win the Premier League title. With England, he would be playing in the qualifiers for World Cup 2018. There were lots of exciting challenges ahead.

'I need to make things right!' Harry told himself.

CHAPTER 22

TOTTENHAM FOR THE TITLE?

'Argggghhhhhhhhhhhhhhhhhhh!' Harry screamed as he lay down on the turf. He tried to stay calm but it felt like really bad news. As he waved for the physio, the pain got worse and worse. White Hart Lane went quiet. The Spurs fans waited nervously to see whether their star striker could carry on.

'You're not singing anymore!' the opposing Sunderland fans cheered bitterly.

If only Harry hadn't slid in for the tackle. Tottenham were already winning 1–0 thanks to his goal. That was his job: scoring goals, not making tackles. But Harry always worked hard for the team. As he went to block the Sunderland centre-back, his

right ankle twisted awkwardly in the grass. If the
injury wasn't too serious, Harry promised himself
that he would never defend again.

Unfortunately, it *was* serious. Harry tried to get
up and play on but that wasn't possible. He hobbled
over to the touchline and sat down again. The Spurs
fans cheered and clapped their hero but Harry's
match was over. He was carried down the tunnel on
a stretcher.

'There's good news and there's bad news,' the
doctor told him after the X-rays. 'The good news is
that there's no fracture. The bad news is that there's
ligament damage.'

Harry wasn't a medical expert but he knew that
'ligament damage' meant no football for a while.
'How long will I be out of action?' he asked, fearing a
big number.

'It's too early to say but you should prepare
yourself for eight weeks out. Hopefully, it won't be
that long.'

Eight weeks! If everything went well, Harry
would be back before December but it was still a big

blow. His 2016–17 season had only just started. He had only played in one Champions League match. Tottenham needed him.

'Who's going to get all our goals now?' he asked.

'Without you hogging all the chances, I'll score loads more!' Dele replied.

It was good to have Katie and his teammates around to cheer Harry up. It was going to be a boring, difficult couple of months for him. He would just have to recover as quickly as possible. To keep himself going, Harry picked out a key date in the calendar: 6 November. The North London Derby – that was what he was aiming for.

'I always score against Arsenal!' Harry reminded everyone.

Thanks to lots of hard work in the gym, he made it just in time. Harry was delighted to be back on the pitch, even if he wasn't at his best. Early in the second half, Tottenham won a penalty and Harry quickly grabbed the ball. It was the perfect chance to get a comeback goal.

He took a long, deep breath and waited for the

referee's whistle. As the Arsenal keeper dived to his left, Harry placed it down the middle.

Goooooooooooooooooaaaaaaaaaaaaaaaalllllllllllllll llllllll!!!!!!!!!!!!!!!!!!!!!!

He was back! Harry pumped his fists at the crowd as his teammates jumped on him.

'What a cool finish!' Son cheered.

Harry didn't last the full match, but he was pleased with his return. 'If I want to win the Golden Boot again, I've got some catching up to do!' he told Pochettino.

Tottenham got knocked out in the Champions League Group Stage, but Harry still had time to grab his first goals in the competition.

'Never mind, we've just got to focus on the Premier League title now,' he told Dele. 'We'll conquer Europe next year!'

After all his goals, Harry became a transfer target for Real Madrid and Manchester United. Tottenham wanted to keep their local hero for as long as possible, so they offered Harry a big new contract until 2020. Saying no didn't even cross his mind.

'I can't leave!' Harry said happily. 'This is my home and we've got trophies to win.'

To celebrate, he went on another scoring spree. Two against Watford, three against West Brom, three against Stoke, two against Everton. By March, he was up to nineteen goals and at the top of the goal-scoring charts again.

'Congratulations, you're back where you belong,' Katie told him.

Harry was pleased but the Premier League title was his number one aim. Spurs were in second place behind Chelsea. Harry would give his all to catch them.

For Harry, winning the 2017 FA Cup was aim number two. In the quarter-finals, Tottenham faced his old club Millwall. So much had changed in the five years since his loan spell there. He would always be grateful to the Lions for their support but that didn't mean he would take it easy on them. Trophies always came first.

As soon as the ball came to him, Harry shot at goal. The Millwall keeper saved it but Harry didn't even notice. He was lying on the grass in agony.

'Is it your right ankle again?' the physio asked after rushing over to him.

Harry just nodded. Was it the same injury all over again? He couldn't bear to think about another eight weeks on the sidelines. He managed to limp off the pitch and down the tunnel. He didn't need to use the stretcher this time and that was a good sign.

'There is ligament damage,' the doctors confirmed, 'but it's not as serious as before. We'll do our best to get you back for the semi-final.'

With a target to aim for, Harry was determined to recover in time. He was back in action two weeks before their big cup match against Chelsea. There was even time for him to score a goal.

'See, I'm feeling sharp!' he promised Pochettino. There was no way that he could miss playing in the FA Cup semi-final. He was a big game player and his team needed him.

The atmosphere at Wembley was electric. As usual, Harry was the second Spurs player out of the tunnel. As he looked up, he could see big blocks of white in the crowd.

'Tottenham! Tottenham! Tottenham!'

If the stadium was this loud for the semi-final, what would the final be like? But Harry couldn't get ahead of himself. He had to focus on beating Chelsea first.

The Blues took the lead but with Harry on the pitch, Spurs were always in the game. He stayed onside at the front post to flick on Christian's low cross. Thanks to his clever touch, the ball flew right into the bottom corner.

Goooooooooooooooooooaaaaaaaaaaaaaaaaaaalllllllllllll llllllllllllllll!!!!!!!!!!!!

'It's like you've got eyes in the back of your head!' Christian cheered as they hugged.

'Why would I need that?' Harry asked. 'The goal doesn't move – it's always in the same place!'

Despite his best efforts, Chelsea scored two late goals to win 4–2. It was very disappointing but Tottenham's season wasn't over yet.

'We've got five Premier League matches left,' Harry told Dele. 'If we can get all fifteen points, the pressure is on Chelsea.'

The first three points came at White Hart Lane in

the North London Derby against Arsenal. Dele got the first goal and Harry scored the second from the penalty spot. The dream was still alive! But at West Ham a week later, Spurs fell apart again. Harry, Dele and Christian tried and tried but they couldn't get the goal they needed. In the second half, Tottenham panicked and conceded a silly goal. The 1-0 defeat left them seven points behind Chelsea.

'No, the title race isn't over yet,' Pochettino told his players. 'Come on, let's finish on a high!'

There was no chance of Harry relaxing. Even if he didn't win the Premier League, he could still win the Golden Boot. He was only three goals behind Everton's Romelu Lukaku with three games to go. Harry closed the gap to two with a neat flick against Manchester United.

'Three goals against Leicester and Hull? I can do that!' he told Dele.

'But what if Lukaku scores again?'

Dele was right; Harry needed to aim even higher. Against Leicester, his first goal was a tap-in, his second was a header and the third was a rocket from the edge of the penalty area. Harry had another amazing hat-trick but he wasn't finished yet. In injury time, he got the ball in the same position and scored again!

Harry was pleased with his four goals but he couldn't help asking himself, 'Why couldn't I do that against West Ham?' He was never satisfied.

Harry would have to think about that later, though. With one game to go, he was on 26 goals and Lukaku was on 24. At the final whistle in the Arsenal vs Everton game, Lukaku was up to 25 goals for Everton thanks to a penalty, but meanwhile Harry was way ahead on 29! With two fantastic finishes and a tap-in, he had grabbed yet another hat-trick against Hull.

'Wow, you were only two goals off the Premier League record,' his proud dad told him. 'And you missed eight games through injury!'

Harry was delighted with his second Golden Boot in a row but it didn't make up for another season without a trophy. Tottenham kept getting so close to glory but would they ever be crowned champions? Harry, the local hero, never stopped believing.

CHAPTER 23

ONE OF EUROPE'S FINEST

Harry jumped up in the England wall but the free kick flew past him and into the top corner. As he watched, his heart sank. Scotland were winning 2–1 at Hampden Park with a few minutes to go.

'Come on, we can't lose this!' Harry shouted to his teammates.

England were unbeaten in qualification for the 2018 World Cup and this, in June 2017, was a key match against their British rivals. It was also Harry's first match as the national captain. For all of these reasons, he refused to let it end in an embarrassing defeat.

With seconds to go, Kyle Walker passed to Raheem Sterling on the left wing. Harry was surrounded by Scottish defenders but he was clever enough to escape. The centre-backs watched Raheem's high cross sail over their heads and thought they were safe. But they weren't. They had missed Harry's brilliant run to the back post.

There wasn't enough time or space to take a touch, so Harry went for a side-foot volley. With incredible technique and composure, he guided his shot past the keeper.

Gooooooooooooooooooooaaaaaaaaaaaalllllllllllllllll lllll!!!!!!!!!!!!!!

It was another big goal in a big game. Under pressure, Harry hardly ever failed.

'You're a born leader,' England manager Gareth Southgate told him after the match. 'That's why I gave you the captain's armband.'

At twenty-four, Harry wasn't a bright young talent anymore. After three excellent seasons, he was now an experienced player with lots of responsibility for club and country. Now he felt ready to take the next step and become one of Europe's finest.

'I might not have as much skill as Cristiano Ronaldo and Lionel Messi but I can score as many goals,' he told Dele.

Harry was full of ambition ahead of the 2017–18 season. It was time to shine in the Champions League as well as the Premier League. But first, he had to get August out of the way.

'Maybe I should just take the month off!' Harry joked at home with Katie.

No matter how hard he tried and how many shots he took, he just couldn't score. He was trying to ignore all the talk about his August goal curse. Their beautiful baby daughter was certainly helping to take his mind off things.

'Yes, you could stay home and change Ivy's nappies with me!' Katie replied with a smile. She knew that Harry could never stay away from football. He loved it so much.

On 1 September, he travelled with England to play against Malta. 'Don't worry, I've got this,' he told his teammates. 'August is over!'

As Dele twisted and turned in the penalty area, Harry got into space and called for the pass. The goalkeeper rushed out but he calmly slotted the ball into the net.

Goooooooooooooooooooaaaaaaaaaaaaaaaalllllllllllllllll llllllll!!!!!!!!!!!!!!!!!!

On the touchline, Southgate pumped his fists. Tottenham fans all over the world did the same. Their goal machine was back.

'Finally!' Dele teased him. 'What would you do without me?'

Harry was too relieved to fight back. 'Thanks, you're the best!' he replied.

Once he scored one, Harry usually scored two. He did it against Malta and then he did it against Everton in the Premier League. As always, Harry's timing was perfect. Tottenham were about to start their Champions League campaign against German giants Borussia Dortmund.

'They picked the wrong time to face me!' he said confidently.

Harry won the ball on the halfway line, headed it forward and chased after it. He wasn't letting anyone get in his way. As he entered the Dortmund penalty area, the defender tried to push him wide. Harry didn't mind; he could score from any angle! Before the keeper could react, the ball flew past him.

The Tottenham fans went wild.

He's one of our own,
He's one of our own,
Harry Kane – he's one of our own!

Harry went hunting for another goal and he got it.

'He just gets better and better!' the commentator marvelled.

It was Harry's first Champions League double, but he wanted a third. He was always hungry for more goals. With a few minutes to go, Pochettino took him off.

'The hat-trick will have to wait until next week!' he told his star striker, patting him on the back.

The APOEL Nicosia defence was prepared for Harry's arrival but there was nothing that they could do to stop him. He made it look so easy. He scored his first goal with his left foot and the second with his right. There was half an hour left to get his third but he only needed five minutes.

Kieran Trippier curled the ball in from the right and Harry ran from the edge of the box to glance it down into the bottom corner. All that heading practice had been worth it.

Gooooooooooooooooooooooooaaaaaaaaaaaaaaaallllllll lllllllllllllllll!!!!!!!!!!!!!!

Harry ran towards Kieran and gave him a big hug. He was always grateful for the assists but this one was particularly special. Harry had his first ever Champions League hat-trick.

'That was perfect!' he told Son afterwards, clutching the match ball tightly.

'Yeah, it was a good win,' his teammate replied.

'No, I mean it was a perfect hat-trick,' Harry explained. 'One with my right foot, one with my left, and one with my head. That's the first time I've ever done that!'

Son laughed. 'You score so many goals. How can you remember them all?'

Every single goal was important to Harry and he often watched videos of his matches to help him improve. He never stopped working on his game.

'Is Kane the best striker in Europe right now?' the newspapers asked. Harry had already scored thirty-six goals by September and he still had three months of the year to go!

To keep his feet on the ground, Harry thought back to his early football days. Arsenal had rejected him and Tottenham had nearly done the same. As an eleven-year-old boy, he had told his hero David Beckham that he wanted to play at Wembley for England. Thanks to lots of practice and determination, Harry had achieved that dream and so much more.

His shirt now hung next to Becks' shirt in the hallway at Chingford Foundation School. Harry had the future at his goalscoring feet. He would do everything possible to lead England to World Cup glory in Russia. But before that, Harry was still determined to win trophies with his boyhood club, Tottenham.

Turn the page for a sneak preview of
another brilliant football story by
Matt and Tom Oldfield. . .

BALE

Available now!

CHAPTER 1

ANFIELD FAREWELL

2 September, 2013

'*El nuevo jugador de Real Madrid, Gareth Bale*'

'Real Madrid's new player, Gareth Bale'.

When they called out his name, the stadium went wild. Thousands of fans clapped and cheered their new record signing. '*Bale! Bale! Bale!*' They chanted his name, the name that many of them already had on their shirts. Gareth couldn't believe it – this wasn't even his debut. He wasn't out there flying down the wing; he was wearing a suit. He could only guess how amazing the atmosphere would be for a game. As he got to his feet and walked up to the stage, he took a long, deep breath and told himself to stay calm. He was no longer the shy boy he once was, but he wasn't yet used to this kind of attention.

But even the butterflies in his stomach couldn't stop the big smile on Gareth's face. This was it; the biggest club in the world and the home of the 'Galácticos', the biggest superstars in the world. Luis Figo, Ronaldo, Raul, David Beckham, Cristiano Ronaldo … and now Gareth Bale. As a child, he'd sat with his father in the stands at local Ninian Park watching his Uncle Chris play, pretending that it was the Bernabéu stadium and that the Cardiff City team was the mighty Real Madrid. Now he was living out that fantasy and this time it was Gareth, not his uncle, who was the star.

As he approached the microphone, Gareth waved to the fans and then to his loved ones. It meant the world to him that they were all here for his big day: his mother Debbie and his father Frank, Granddad Dennis, his older sister Vicky, his best friend Ellis and, of course, his girlfriend Emma and their beautiful young daughter Alba. Without their endless support, he knew he would never have made it here.

When things settled down a bit, Gareth began:

'Es un sueño para mi jugar para Real Madrid.

Gracias por esta gran acogida. ¡Hala Madrid!'

These were the first Spanish words he'd learnt and, of course, the most important. He'd practised them for days so that even in the excitement, he wouldn't forget them: 'It's my dream to play for Real Madrid. Thank you for this big welcome. Come on Madrid!' The noise was incredible, so loud that he'd had to pause halfway through.

And then came the moment everyone had been waiting for, especially Gareth. He'd imagined it so many times but this time it was real. The President of Real Madrid held up the famous white shirt and there was his name in big black letters across the back: 'BALE'. The cameras flashed and the crowd roared once more. He was a Galáctico now – the most expensive of them all – and so his old Number 3 was no longer good enough. As he had in his last season at Tottenham, now he wore the number of his childhood hero, the Manchester United wing wizard Ryan Giggs – 11.

Michael Owen had worn the number at Real Madrid in 2004, as had Arjen Robben in 2007. Gareth was proud to follow in their footsteps but he was determined to make that shirt his own. Watching the scenes around him, Gareth couldn't wait for the biggest challenge of his life. He was the most expensive player in the world and there would be a lot of pressure on him to join his teammate Cristiano Ronaldo as one of the very best players of all time.

As he did keepie-uppies on the Bernabéu pitch, Gareth thought back to his childhood days at Caedelyn Park. As a lightning-fast teenager in Wales, his family and coaches had predicted big things for him but no-one had predicted this. At both Southampton and Tottenham, there had been difficult times when injuries looked like they might end Gareth's childhood dream. But the Welsh dragon had battled on and made it to the top.

Individual

🏆 PFA Young Player of the Year: 2014–15

🏆 Premier League PFA Team of the Year: 2014–15, 2015–16, 2016–17

🏆 Premier League Golden Boot: 2015–16, 2016–17

KANE

(10) THE FACTS

NAME: HARRY EDWARD KANE

DATE OF BIRTH: 28 July 1993

AGE: 24

PLACE OF BIRTH: Walthamstow, London

NATIONALITY: England

BEST FRIEND: Dele Alli

CURRENT CLUB: Tottenham

POSITION: ST

THE STATS

Height (cm):	**188**
Club appearances:	**239**
Club goals:	**126**
Club trophies:	**0**
International appearances:	**23**
International goals:	**12**
International trophies:	**0**
Ballon d'Ors:	**0**

★ ★ ★ **HERO RATING: 88** ★ ★ ★

GREATEST MOMENTS

7 APRIL 2014,
TOTTENHAM 5-1 SUNDERLAND

Harry's first Premier League goal was a long time coming. After four loan spells, he finally got his chance at Tottenham under Tim Sherwood. Against Sunderland, Christian Eriksen curled a brilliant ball into the six-yard box and Harry beat his marker to score. It was a real striker's finish and a sign of the great things to come.

2 NOVEMBER 2014, ASTON VILLA 1-2 TOTTENHAM

This was the goal that changed Harry's career at White Hart Lane. He has definitely scored better goals but this last-minute free kick won the match for Tottenham. Before this, Harry was a substitute. After this, he became the star striker we know and love.

7 FEBRUARY 2015, TOTTENHAM 2-1 ARSENAL

This was the day that Harry became a true Tottenham hero. In the big North London Derby, he scored two goals to secure a famous victory. Harry's first goal was a tap-in but the second was a world-class header. He used his power and technique to direct the ball right into the corner of the Arsenal goal.

19 MARCH 2015, ENGLAND 4-0 LITHUANIA

It was Harry's international debut at Wembley and he had only been on the pitch for 80 seconds. Raheem Sterling crossed from the left and, as usual, Harry was in the right place at the right time. He scored with a simple header at the back post and then bumped into the match official!

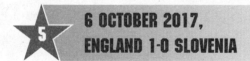

6 OCTOBER 2017, ENGLAND 1-0 SLOVENIA

On a tense night at Wembley, the new England captain led his country to the 2018 World Cup in Russia. In the last minute, Kyle Walker crossed from the right and Harry stretched out his lethal right leg to poke the ball past the keeper.

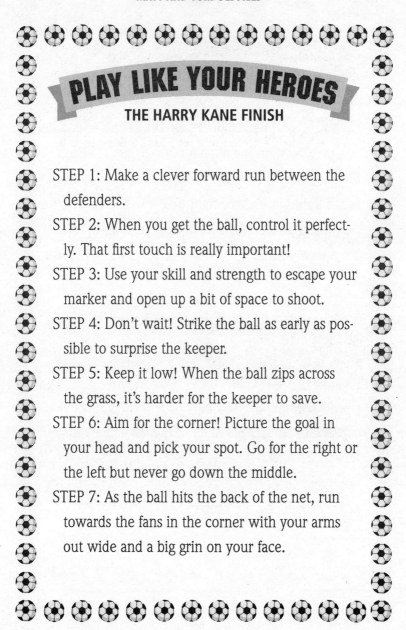

PLAY LIKE YOUR HEROES

THE HARRY KANE FINISH

STEP 1: Make a clever forward run between the defenders.

STEP 2: When you get the ball, control it perfectly. That first touch is really important!

STEP 3: Use your skill and strength to escape your marker and open up a bit of space to shoot.

STEP 4: Don't wait! Strike the ball as early as possible to surprise the keeper.

STEP 5: Keep it low! When the ball zips across the grass, it's harder for the keeper to save.

STEP 6: Aim for the corner! Picture the goal in your head and pick your spot. Go for the right or the left but never go down the middle.

STEP 7: As the ball hits the back of the net, run towards the fans in the corner with your arms out wide and a big grin on your face.

TEST YOUR KNOWLEDGE

QUESTIONS

1. Who was Harry's first Tottenham hero?

2. What position did Harry first play at Ridgeway Rovers?

3. Which other England legend also played for Ridgeway Rovers?

4. Which three clubs did Harry have trials with when he was a youngster?

5. Name three of Harry's teammates in the Tottenham youth team.

6. How many loan spells did Harry have before settling at Spurs?

7. Who was the Spurs manager when Harry made his first Premier League start?

8. Who gave Harry his Number 18 shirt when he left Tottenham?

9. Harry scored on his England debut – True or False?

10. How many goals did Harry score for England at Euro 2016?

11. How many Premier League Golden Boots has Harry won so far?

Answers below. . . No cheating!

1. *Teddy Sheringham* 2. *Goalkeeper* 3. *David Beckham* 4. *Arsenal, Watford and Tottenham* 5. *Any of Tom Carroll, Jonathan Obika, Kudus Oyenuga, Ryan Mason, Andros Townsend and Steven Caulker* 6. *Four – Leyton Orient, Millwall, Norwich City and Leicester City* 7. *Tim Sherwood* 8. *Jermain Defoe* 9. *True – Harry scored after only 80 seconds against Lithuania!* 10. *0* 11. *2*

HAVE YOU GOT THEM ALL?

FOOTBALL HEROES